BLOOD MONEY

DINERO DE SANGRE BOOK 1

LANA SKY

Blood Money

Blood Money By Lana Sky

Cover Design and Interior Formatting by Charity Chimni
Editing and Proofreading by Charity Chimni

ISBN: 978-1-956608-08-3

ACKNOWLEDGMENTS

Thanks so much to everyone who supported this draft along the way, including the many beta readers who provided encouragement! Please keep in mind that this story includes dark, graphic and explicit content matter that is not suitable for readers under the age of 18—or for readers who are uncomfortable with the following subject matter: explicit sex, mentions of sexual abuse, mentions of child abuse, mentions of eating disorders, graphic depictions of violence, and mentions of self-harm.

People always laughed when they heard his name, Domino. Paired with his unique attire and penchant for straw cowboy hats, the moniker attributed to his unique allure as a bodyguard. As a result, people rarely took him seriously upon their first meeting.

Who does this motherfucker think he is? Skeptical men would sometimes ask that very question while strolling from my father's office—all while Domino himself would watch quietly from the sidelines of the sprawling boardroom they'd been summoned to.

The next time they were ever seen again would be in pieces, grimly documented by a medical examiner called to investigate the cause of death. Most determinations were just guesses, of course—*wood chipper accident, bear attack,* and the average *sky diving mishap.*

My father controlled the police commissioner, so the official reason didn't really matter. It could be as outlandish as "tiger mauling," and no one ever batted an eye. So was the hold the Pavalos family had over Terra Rodea—at least until the day my family was upended and Domino, that faithful soldier, set his sights on *me*.

Killing me would have been merciful on his end. Even a supposed wild bear attack would have been a better ending than the one he had in mind.

I never knew the extent of the hatred such a man could harbor.

I never knew the violence one human soul could be capable of.

I never realized that, when it came to destroying my father and toppling his million-dollar empire, Domino's price would have been relatively low in the grand scheme.

To betray my family, Domino Valenciaga requested only one thing.

Me.

CHAPTER ONE

He's late.

I try not to dwell on the potential explanations, or the fact that every passing second he delays risks us losing the reservation it took months to secure. It's just ten minutes past our scheduled meeting time of six. So what if he hasn't been answering his phone since then, either?

I know what—he has his dick in someone else.

Though, I shouldn't dwell on that. *Utilize your coping mechanisms more*, my therapist liked to harp. The main one she touted was counting to five whenever the anxiety started to build. *Ground yourself, Ada. Think of one positive to go along with every breath.*

One.

I'm wearing the new Alexander Marenti summer design from his exclusive collection, and it shows off my body well.

Two.

I hate this stupid dress.

Three.

Daddy got it only as a pity offering for missing my birthday dinner—and only on the say-so of that cunt bitch secretary of his who handled all of his afterthought social obligations these days.

Four.

Tristan's fucking Alexi again.

Five.

He's balls deep within that whore, and that's why he's late. If he shows up now, it will only prove me right. Again. The bastard can only last exactly six-point-seven minutes with an extra wasted to button-up his shitty chinos—

"Hey, baby!"

Someone grabs me from behind, sliding their hands along my hips, and I smother a hiss of disgust. Tristan. His cloying cologne gives him away, and I force my lips into a smile. "Hey, baby."

My nostrils flare as I spin to face him, and I nearly choke. He reeks of that signature cologne—more so than usual. As if he dumped half the bottle over himself to disguise the stench of Alexi's shitty perfume and their eight-minute sex session.

I note that his pink lips are unusually wet as well, his dark hair playfully tousled.

Fuck him.

He's smiling, but it's strained around the edges. Alexi was always a biter from what I've heard, prone to leaving marks that made him wince for days whenever we kissed. It was one of his telltale signs.

I promised not to take him back after the first time.

It's the tenth. Maybe eleventh, but I'm still here, letting him plant a chaste peck on my lips. The way he kisses me when Alexi's taste is on his tongue, and he hasn't popped a breath mint yet.

Fuck. I cross over to the bubbling fountain near the restaurant's entrance. Overall, the courtyard attached to the venue is beautiful enough to justify its long waitlist and hefty prices, with a Spanish design and a manicured garden. The fountain itself is large enough to swim in, sporting a statue of an angel in the center. Briefly, I consider what might happen if I sank to my knees and dunked my head beneath the water's surface. Perhaps for "five minutes" of calm.

Then I imagine how better it would feel to hold Tristan's head down instead.

Objectively, I know how it looks from the outside. For the daughter of Roy Pavalos to chase after some bottom-feeding lawyer who can't keep his dick in his pants where the town whore is concerned.

It's pathetic.

It's strategic. Said bottom-feeding lawyer just so happens to be the one pawn standing in between my father and a potential federal indictment.

I don't love Tristan. He's merely an assignment. My duty to the family.

Fucking me gives him a reason to drag his heels, greasing up the wheels of justice just long enough for Roy Pavalos to find a way out of the mess he created for himself. As thanks, Daddy keeps my debit cards well-funded and pays my car note. Though hell, it's not like I have a choice.

I'm not allowed to seek out my own employment.

I'm not even allowed to book a gyno appointment without his say-so.

Why? Because we are *Pavalos. Pavalos. Pavalos…*

From the day I was born with that goddamn last name, I've been cursed. My life has never been my own. Everything I do, down to the clothing I wear, is with my father's approval. So is the responsibility of being born a Pavalos. At least with a mother like mine who lacked the will to divorce my father for the sake of her children like his prior two wives did. We're both no better than dolls, placed beautifully on a shelf for the world to admire.

"Ada? You okay, baby?"

Tristan slides his hands around my ribcage, ghosting my breasts. It takes everything I have not to cringe from him.

"I'm sorry I'm late," he says, flashing a smile that displays the mouth of beautiful teeth he bought last year with one of my father's bribe payments. "I got held up by work. You ready for dinner? I know this is important to you."

Important. As if he would ever know what truly matters in my world. I don't even have that privilege.

Still, I smile and preen the way I've been taught my whole life. If I'm a marionette on strings, my mother, Lia Pavalos, is the expert porcelain doll. By the time she married my father, the woman had refined how to present a vision of perfection to the public. How to lie. How to sleep with a man who regularly fucks another and how to look amazing while doing so.

"I'm fine," I say. In fact, I never stopped smiling. "Let's go eat," I add, linking my arm through his. "I'm starving."

In reality, I haven't eaten a solid meal since Monday. It's Friday. That's nearly a full week, but nowhere near close to my record. The hunger gnawing at my stomach is a constant distraction, battling with everything else fighting for my attention at the present—and ignoring it might be the one damn thing I'm allowed to do without input from anyone else. I can pick when to silence my twisting, growling stomach, and when not to.

Tonight, I'll make myself try some crackers, at least. Maybe some fish.

I'm fine.

In a place so beautiful, how could I not be?

The restaurant's interior is lavishly furnished with walls an emerald-green and black marble floors. I forget the establishment's name, but it's something gloriously Spanish, and it's a perfect setting to serve as the stage upon which I'll play my role in the Pavalos family tonight.

That as the perfect daughter with the perfect boyfriend, on a perfect evening without a care in the world; it doesn't matter that every damn aspect of it is a lie.

"You've barely eaten your food," Tristan says once we've been seated and served. It all passed in a blur; I don't even remember what I ordered.

Soup, it seems, a nice contrast to Tristan's perfectly seared steak.

"What do you mean? It's delicious!" I make a show of prodding at the dish before me, composed of chunks of carrots and potato—Porrusalda, I think it's called—but I'm too preoccupied to even put on a convincing act. The press and the paparazzi are watching. After all, tonight's guest list has been coincidentally tailored so that everyone in this city who matters happens to be dining right here and right now. My father planned it this way, I'm sure. Even something as simple as a date has been carefully crafted to his benefit.

And that's the catch.

By tomorrow he will be arrested for murder, and no fancy dinner will be able to change that narrative. What a way for it all to end. For decades he spent his life playing the city as a chessboard, but this is one game that he won't dominate. We're already in checkmate.

"I know I haven't been the best lately," Tristan declares, reaching over to grab my hand. "I can tell you're upset."

I force a laugh. "I'm fine, really." Inside, I'm shaking, wondering what gave me away. I've spent six months of this relationship faking and faking and *faking*. I don't think he's ever caught on once, or maybe I've just been too wrapped up in myself to notice.

Now, he's eyeing me in a way he hasn't before, with his blue eyes narrowed over my face. Ironically, he looks like a lawyer, and I guess he must be a damn good one considering how badly my father wanted to extend his influence over him.

"I know I fucked up." The intensity in his voice catches me off guard. "I know I did. I promise that next time I'll be better. I won't let it happen again."

"You mean you won't fall into Alexi's bed again," I say, snatching a piece of bread from the customary basket resting between us. It's some fancy, flaky artisan style, and it tastes like ashes as I choke down a bite.

"Ada…" Tristan's cheeks flush, eyes widening with guilt, but I don't feel like having this conversation right now. In the grand scheme, I'm not even that upset. I was never invested in this relationship. Tristan isn't my type, but there's still the principle of the matter. The man is lucky enough to date the daughter of Roy Pavalos, and yet he still can't stop sleeping with a trailer trash whore.

"You should eat," I say, smiling wider. "I'm sure you can't stay long, what with your busy schedule."

"You always do this," Tristan says, setting his silverware down noisily.

I raise an eyebrow, and he continues, "Shut me down. You never talk about anything, not even yourself. Sometimes it's like dating the wall."

A wall or maybe a doll? It's simply the way I was raised to be. To always perform my pretty perfect role.

Until now. I could blame the wine, or the fact that I'm drinking on an empty stomach. Regardless, words bubble up before I can hold them at bay. "I'm not quite as stupid as I look, you do realize." I don't recognize the hard tone—or maybe I do, just in a very different pitch. My father speaks this way. Bluntly and cold. "I know you've been fucking her. Frankly, I haven't cared, but if you could be a little more discreet about it, I'd appreciate that."

He blinks. "Baby, I—"

"I think I want the flan for dessert," I say with my best smile, snatching a leather-bound menu. "We can pose for a picture of you feeding me a bite—"

"This is something we should talk about, Ada. You know, like a real couple?"

He has the nerve to sound so earnest. As if he doesn't know damn well what this really is. Not a relationship, but a business transaction.

"You were promoted to partner a month after dating me," I point out absently. "Don't tell me you believe that was solely on your merits as an amazing lawyer."

He frowns. I've insulted him. Good.

Wadding up my napkin, I set it aside and make eye contact with a passing waiter. "More wine," I tell him.

"Baby, I think you've had enough."

"I'll tell you when I've had enough," I say, grabbing my near-empty glass. I drain it with one hard pull and relish the liquid dripping down my throat.

My father enjoys the same vices. In reality, we're far more alike than either of us would care to admit. It's why he kept me close, long after he's shoved Pablo and Demelio—his two sons from a previous marriage—from his life. They challenged him. They took offense to his vicious actions and tyrannical ways with money. They had morals.

Souls.

They also had two different mothers from mine. Mine, Lia, is Roy's third wife and least impressive. The modest, religious daughter of a judge, she gave Roy a softer public edge than his previous debutante bride or the beauty queen with a penchant for charity he left her for.

Lia humbled me, he likes to say. Humbled him the way fire humbled the Devil. She merely gave credence to his more self-deprecating attributes. Before her, he blamed his problems on liquor and cocaine. Now? He blames God, disguising his viler acts behind a repentant sinner's façade.

"…don't know what's gotten into you," Tristan is murmuring, once I bother to pay attention to him again.

Into me. How would he know? He's never known the real me. I've always been a grinning puppet on his arm, or a perky sex doll.

The reality of who I am is a mash of far different descriptors. Liquor, cocaine, and laxatives. My vice arsenal.

In this moment, I crave all three. I'm not upset about Tristan—I'm not. It's how damn hot it is in this supposedly grand establishment. It's how bright the lights are. It's the fact that my arraignment outfit is already picked out.

The fact that I've been practicing my lines in the mirror for the moment I'm inevitably interviewed by the police. The fact that I've already programmed the state penitentiary number into my cell phone with the understanding that soon enough, calls from that building will dictate my entire life.

I might as well be imprisoned there, too, though the thought is far more appealing than I suppose it should be. Ironically, I'd have far more freedom behind bars.

"Ada? I think we really need to talk. There's something—"

"I need to use the bathroom," I say, rising to my feet. That piece of bread weighs on my stomach. I feel too heavy. Dirty. Unclean. My mother instructs the maids to clean the floors seven times a day.

Is this really so different?

"Ada, wait." He grabs my hand, and I just eye it, feeling detached from the slim, manicured fingers in his grasp. These hands have done things my mind can never comprehend. Vicious, vile, disgusting things.

All in the name of family.

"Ada? Fine, if you want to do this now, I'll come clean. I know about the indictment."

Blood rushes through my ears in a torrent of deafening noise. When I blink, Tristan's lips are still moving, forcing my brain to play catch up to understand.

"W-What?"

"I know, baby," he says gently. "Why do you think I was really late? I was busting my ass to make sure the goddamn reporters wouldn't try to catch you here alone. I know you're worried. And I could lose my job for this, but…it's been squashed. I don't know how, but according to my contacts at the precinct, the warrant to arrest your father has been put on indefinite hold. I can't get any answers as to why. Maybe they jumped the gun—"

"What do you mean?"

"Your father won't be arrested tomorrow, baby." He rises to his feet, pulling me into his arms. I think he's genuinely surprised when I wrench away. "What's wrong?"

My smile is gone, replaced by a look that haunts me in the polished reflective wall across from our table—one of abject horror.

Daddy won't be hauled off to jail tomorrow, plunging our family into international public scandal and turmoil.

I won't have to wear my chosen black dress or practice my "sad face" in the mirror for hours before facing the press.

I won't have to fear getting a call from the state pen every day.

Roy Pavalos will stay in my home. In my life.

Controlling my world with an iron fist.

"I need to use the bathroom." I twist out of Tristan's reach, staggering in the direction of the restrooms.

"Wait—" he grabs my arm, displaying a persistence he rarely has. "There's something else. I want you to come away with me. Tonight. I've already made the arrangements, and we can—"

"What?" I'm barely listening to him.

A flicker of movement catches my eye from across the room near the window. Or where the window once was. A hole is there now. Before it, a dance of swirling glass floats through the air, suspended for a second that seems frozen in time.

Then an explosion of noise sends everything moving again. *Boom!* People start screaming. Running. Dazed, I look back at Tristan, but he's not there anymore…

Or at least he's not on his feet.

My brain takes ages to connect the dots with the red liquid splattered all over the floor and the body lying nearby. Except it's not right. Can't be Tristan—the proportions are all wrong. There are two arms, two legs, a torso, but no head…

I'm aware that my mouth is open, but no words come out.

All I can do is stare.

Then run. It's an instinctive motion, pivoting on my heel, to join the press of people racing for the nearest exit. There's no rhyme or reason to it. No thinking.

I make it so easy for the man who must have been standing behind me all along, waiting to attack.

I see his fist come from nowhere and realize that nothing I can do will stop it from colliding with my skull.

The sickening thud that comes next, somehow sounds more violent than the previous noise that shattered the quiet atmosphere.

And the world goes black.

CHAPTER TWO

Some men wear their intentions so blatantly. You can look them in the eye and see every thought in their head rattling around, as legible as newspaper headlines.

In my world, the only things that matter are what could make a splashy news story, after all.

People love the sordid nature of my father's political career—a rags to riches fairy tale and a shining example of hard work. And ambition. Everyone ignores the darker side of his inspiring story, like the supposed cartel ties that catapulted him to power, or the origin of the money that funds his decade-long political run. They love the mystery of who he's fucking and what business move he might make next. The flashy stuff.

No one cares that he's a true monster. That he rules the lives of those around him with an iron fist. That he's cruel and volatile with a temper to match his ambition.

Frankly, those details are boring, the stuff everyone already knows. Men with power have secrets. They live double lives and aren't nearly as perfect as they want the world to believe.

My life certainly wasn't perfect. I think all of us knew that there was always a time limit ruthlessly ticking the seconds down until it all fell apart. You can only live on blood money for so long before the lies and secrets start to catch up.

Ours are plenty, locked away in a closet so full of skeletons it might as well be a crypt. My father had a way of justifying it all. For the sake of the family.

For my mother.

For me.

We were tethered to him beyond any familial ties.

He ensured as much. From the age of fifteen, I ceased to be his daughter, Ada-Maria Lucia Pavalos.

I became his accomplice. For years, every sick, sordid undertaking of his has stained my soul. I couldn't plead ignorance if I tried.

The day he went to federal prison, I wouldn't be far behind him.

But now, I don't have to worry about that possibility anymore—*I'm dead.*

As my awareness returns in bits and pieces, my first coherent thought is that I wish my head had been the one blown apart. Not Tristan's.

I know that for certain—his body was the one lying on the floor. Someone killed him.

Though, hell, maybe I've gotten my wish after all—they're just a poor shot and failed to kill me outright. My skull is on fire, every movement resonating like a kick to the head. I'd scream if I could, but my lips remain frozen, clamped together.

Am I paralyzed?

Or drugged?

I should know the difference…

"…she's a sexy piece of ass, ain't she?" The voice drips into my skull, uttered gruffly, but I don't recognize the speaker. A male. Fear drips through my veins, fighting to wake up my sleeping nerves and lifeless muscles.

Nausea rips through me, and I can feel the impulse to vomit. Purge. Reset.

But I can't.

"Don't touch her," another man replies. His voice is softer, and I strain to make it out more clearly. They sound close, but muffled, as if I'm hearing them from underwater. "Dom said she was his alone. No marks. No injuries. You better pray you didn't bruise her with that punch—"

"If he wanted her scot-free, then the bastard should have gotten her himself. We did all the fucking work and brought her out here, to the middle of fucking nowhere. Why not have a little taste? If he plans on doing to the little witch what he's done to the rest, it would be a damn shame to let this sexy bitch go to waste."

The rest…

"I've warned you, Trey," the second man replies. "He said we can't touch her."

My body is moved without any action on my part, and I land heavily on something solid and unyielding. A floor? It's colder than the tile in my bathroom. Marble?

Not the flooring of the restaurant, I suspect.

Where the hell am I?

Sensation is returning to the rest of my body, at least, in excruciatingly slow increments. The pain in my head is centered along my right temple—but that's the least of my worries.

Harsh, an unfamiliar touch grazes my thigh, inching beneath the hemline of my dress. Higher. Too high. Boldly, they shove my panties aside, prodding the flesh beneath the lace barrier. Horror rises up so fiercely I can taste it—but I'm paralyzed, unable to control my limbs, even to flinch. My eyelids are too heavy to lift. I can't even speak.

"Damn," the gruffer of the two men breathes, sounding sickeningly close. "She's like a goddamn little furnace—"

"Enough." That voice is unlike the others. Instantly, I recognize it. The guttural baritone shoots through me, triggering a sensation few men have ever inspired.

It takes a lot to scare the daughter of Roy Pavalos. My childhood was filled with inviting criminals and drug dealers over for dinner. My teenage years were spent in their beds, and all the while my father lorded over every single interaction like a tyrant king.

But it's rare to meet someone that truly sends a shiver through my core. In fact, I think only one man has ever fit the bill.

Domino Valenciaga.

He had an accent retained from a past no one knew anything about. Something from Latin America, maybe Portuguese, or Brazilian. The slight inflection turned every word he said into a double-edged sword, musical almost. Lethal in another sense. He was the only person I ever knew to make a death sentence sound beautiful.

For five years, he's been my father's righthand man, recruited from only God knows where, standing faithfully by his side ever since.

A funny thought comes to me now, despite the stench of blood in my nostrils and the fear pummeling through my chest like a barrage of blows—I've rarely spoken to him directly, apart from the typical greeting.

"Hello," I'd say.

His reply was always the same. *"Ada-Maria."*

It's a strange admission now, but I used to have nightmares, starring the very specific way he could say my name, mangling the two syllables into one unique utterance. "Nightmares" that left me so wet I had to relieve the ache with my own fingers.

It's his voice I'm hearing now, though he's speaking too quickly, and my head hurts too badly to follow. I only catch snippets.

"…blood. You killed him in front of her?" Domino asks. His speech is so flat that one can never get a read on his emotions. I've heard him praise my father and curse his enemies, all while sounding no different.

What is he doing here?

"Didn't have a choice," the second of the two men explains. "You wanted him dead. The bastard hired elite security. The restaurant was the only way."

Wanted him dead.

I keep seeing flashes of Tristan. His eyes. His face. His body lying prone on the ground, covered in blood.

A wave of panic drowns me in terror. I don't know how my body remains so still, each breath slow and heavy. Whatever drug they gave me, it's damn good.

So good, I almost give in to the mind-numbing calm that smothers most of my thoughts. Why fight? It feels better to be high…

"Still, you killed him in front of her," Domino says. "That might complicate matters. I aimed to use her ignorance to my advantage. Now she'll have an idea of the danger she's in."

Danger?

"You didn't say not to fucking kill no one in front of this bitch," the first speaker interjects, his brashness clashing harshly with Domino's suave monotone.

The drug in my system is strong—definitely a sedative—but it must be wearing off. All at once, sensation returns to my face, enough that I can flutter my eyelids, gleaning snatches of my surroundings snippets at a time.

I'm in a room, I think. Somewhere with dim lighting. Blinking is a struggle, turning my perception of the world into a disjointed slide show.

I see a shadow. A man? He moves quickly, growing larger by the second.

My heart races as a smell itches my nostrils, mingling with the stench of blood. Spice. Masculine musk. Lethality.

"No," Domino replies, his voice washing over me as that shadow becomes even larger. Him? "But do you know what I *did* ask you to do?"

My belly flips, picking up on the slow, subtle inflection that colors his usually emotionless voice.

"I asked you not to touch her."

"We had to carry her in here," the man argues. "Didn't we—"

"That's not what I meant. Two fingers. That's how many you shoved inside of her cunt just now, am I correct? Not to mention what you've done to her face."

A whoosh of air breezes past my head, triggering another wave of nausea. I can physically gag—and at the same time, I'm able to keep my eyes open for longer than a second.

The man standing before me is the devil, I'm sure of it. My mother spent enough of my childhood peppering my bedtimes with stories of the creature awaiting me if I dared to sin. The only problem?

I'd been born into sin, committing my first immoral act the second I'd been given the name Pavalos. This family is evil incarnate, my life an endless parade of sin after sin.

But if I ever felt the need to repent, it would be now.

The devil is a cold soul with dark eyes devoid of compassion or warmth. They stare at something beyond me, set in a face so beautiful it could only belong to a fallen angel who dared to forsake God himself.

Dazed, I realize that I've seen this face before—every day, in fact, for the past five years. He's certainly no angel, just a man with the beauty of a divine being.

Domino Valenciaga.

"Apologies, if I didn't make myself clear, before," he says, his voice so soft, his demeanor so casual—which makes the fact that he draws a blade from a sheath strapped to his belt all the more terrifying.

My father loved that gimmick of his. While his compatriots hired private guards armed with military-grade weapons, *his* man required only a blade, one that he displayed openly from a battered leather sheath he kept on his belt, no matter the outfit or occasion.

The unique weapon gave him an air of mystery, and made him unpredictable in a world based on surefire odds and getting one over on an opponent.

My father liked to call Domino his wildcard. His ace in the hole. His berserker.

As disoriented as I am, I can see why. He's riveting as the light reflects off his blade and highlights the lone glint in his eye that proves without a shadow of a doubt... He's soulless. An animal relying purely on instinct.

The will to kill comes as easy to him as breathing.

"I told you she was mine." His tone remains so level that the knife in his hand could be as trivial as a cigar. Something held merely to pass the time.

Until he crosses beyond my line of sight with a slow, easy stride.

A noise echoes next, so chilling that it snaps what remnants of the drug are still controlling my ability to move. I flinch, rolling onto my back with a better view of the ceiling above and the room's layout overall.

It's spacious, but I don't recognize the color scheme. Beige walls. A high, white ceiling.

And red liquid spraying in an arch as if by some new age fountain—or in this case, from a man clutching his right arm to his chest as he staggers into my line of view.

I've never heard someone scream like this.

Liar. But it's a sound I've tried my damned hardest to suppress.

The cry of a man in pain is so different from any other. So guttural, almost a howl—but it's the squeal you watch out for. That high-pitched inflection point that heralds true pain.

This man is nowhere near there. Yet. "What the fuck—"

"Raise your hand," Domino says.

My head lolls toward the sound of his voice and I find him, standing tall just a few steps away. He tosses his knife into the air, catching it by the handle easily. There's no mark on the blade, but it's the only weapon capable of causing so much blood…

"Do what he says," another man warns. He's too far back for me to see his face. I only catch a shadow from the corner of my eye.

"Your hand," Domino requests, snapping his fingers. "Lift it."

Still groaning, the other man complies, revealing fingers streaked in scarlet that tremble with agony. A gash slices into the flesh of his forearm, the source of the bleeding.

I am *so* high. The lighting plays off my vision, turning every drop of scarlet into a blazing, flickering trail like neon paint. It drips, drips, drips as Domino inspects the limb, his face unreadable from this angle.

Then he moves in a way that resembles some sick, beautiful dance. Without warning, he grabs the man's arm, ignoring how he whines as a result. Then he brandishes the knife.

The man sputters, "N-No—"

My eyelids fall, drenching me in darkness. I don't see the action that results in the horrific scream that echoes next, but I can guess. Something to do with the blade hitting a firm surface that gives with a crunching squelch.

The screaming takes on an almost musical quality, building to a high-pitched crescendo. Then, *bingo*. There it is. That note of true agony.

The one my father taught me how to play.

Disgust rips through my body, crawling up my throat. I gag so hard I lurch onto my stomach, forced to brace my hands against the floor as liquid issues from my lips. Over and over.

I'm still choking on bile when I sense a flicker of movement come from behind.

"Two fingers for the two you used to soil what is mine," Domino says. "Now get the fuck out. You—" his shift in tone makes me suspect he's speaking to the other man beyond my view. "Take his share and get him out of here. Now."

"Yes, sir."

Footsteps echo off the polished flooring—marble as I suspected, a tan color with white swirls interspersed within the mass—and the screaming grows distant, eventually silenced altogether.

My fear builds unchecked, and I turn my focus inward, fixating on every hair out of place and every throbbing inch of skin.

I think they hit me, whoever they were…

The same men who shot Tristan through the head. A whimpering cry escapes my throat, and I'm startled by the genuine pain in it.

Tristan…

He was a dick, but I've never seen someone shot before.

I've never smelled so much fresh blood.

I guess this means we won't be named the city's "Hottest New Young Couple" in the society pages…

"You're awake." That voice.

I didn't imagine it—or any of this for that matter. It's real. Even in my imagination, I couldn't fake the unique way that baritone deepens when it comes to me.

I focus on my breathing as more control of my limbs returns. I have enough strength to lift my head, viewing the strange room from a different angle.

It resembles a foyer of some sort. Large and circular with a high ceiling and a rounded archway leading off to a shadowed hall up ahead.

It's not the foyer of Casa De Mio, my father's estate. Neither do I recognize the space as belonging to one of his offices or associates. It doesn't even match the background of the restaurant.

Could this property belong to Domino?

"Look at me, Ada-Maria."

I shiver, feeling his voice vibrate through my bones. Somehow, I muster up the energy to crane my neck enough to see him standing over me. He retrieved a cloth from somewhere, using it to leisurely clean off his blade. This time it is streaked with red. Blood.

The color plays off the gold in his skin, enhancing the darkness of those piercing eyes that I've seen reduce men to quivering puddles in an instant.

Something's wrong. That inner voice tickles the back of my skull, growing louder as more realizations register on my tired brain. For one, I don't see my father. I don't hear his loud, booming voice, tinged with the playful accent that added to his charm.

Attempting to speak is a grueling exercise that seems to take hours to put into fruition. In reality, it must only be seconds. "W-Where…is Papa?"

His eyes cut to mine with a ruthless intensity, so sharp that it's like another dose of a far different drug. Fear? It seeps through my veins, ten times stronger than the previous times I shared a room with him.

He takes his time cleaning off his blade before re-sheathing it. "We weren't meant to speak like this," he says, gesturing with his free hand to the room around us. Then he snaps his fingers.

"Yes, sir?" a new voice calls out. A woman's, as foreign to me as the two men were.

"Help Ms. Pavalos get ready for dinner, Ines. The dining room, please. Ten minutes."

"Yes, sir."

Soft footsteps pad in my direction, and I turn toward the archway to find a woman entering through it. She's petite, wearing a gray dress, her hair slicked back. Barring the color of her attire, she could be one of the maids from my father's complex.

She approaches me, stooping to brace her hand against my shoulder. With a surprising amount of strength, she guides me to stand on legs that quiver like jelly.

It hurts to move, even enough to look over my shoulder, but I do, seeking out the figure with his back to me.

I try to speak. "Domino… Domino!"

He retreats through another doorway without a word.

"This way, Miss," Ines says, urging me forward.

Pain shoots up my spine with every step. My hip feels sore and bruised. Only God knows what happened after the restaurant.

Or how long I was unconscious. Between my legs feels damp, and an acrid stench reaches my nose with horrifying implications. Urine?

"This way." The woman guides me through a doorway, and I'm brought face to face with a woman so far from the image she spent thousands presenting to the world that I don't recognize her at first.

It's me.

It's funny that despite everything I've been through, nothing startles me more than seeing myself look like this. My hair is a rat's nest. My dress is torn, and blood streaks my thigh, visible through the slit. More dried blood is encrusted over my right temple, and my mascara is running.

My first impulse is to reach for my purse for my makeup pouch. Papa always prided appearance over all else. No matter what hell I'd been through, my foremost duty is to always look like I deserved to uphold the name Pavalos.

"We have ten minutes," Ines says, tugging at the sleeve of my dress. She has it undone, peeled down to my waist before I remember how to move.

The smell of urine grows stronger, definitely coming from me.

"S-Stop!" I bat her hand away and stagger to the counter, bracing my hands flat against the sturdy surface. "Tristan. I...we need to call the police. Call my father. We need to—"

"We have ten minutes," the woman insists, but there's an urgent edge to her voice that wasn't there before.

Her eyes meet mine over the mirror's surface, an intense shade of brown that gleams like gold.

When she tugs at my dress again, I just let her, sinking into the fog dulling my thoughts. It's been days since I've been on a high like this. The mind-numbing daze where you can just sit back and lose hours at a time. I used to compare the feeling to that of taking a warm bath as a child, with a caring mother to bathe your limbs and wrap you nice and warm in a towel.

But this high is harsher. A literal experience of being stripped naked and bathed by a stranger, doused in sickly sweet perfume, and dressed in an outfit I don't recognize.

Domino. I cling to his name like a raft in a flash flood, fighting to stay above the rushing waves. He's here... For a reason. He brought me here for a reason. But where is my father? And Tristan...

"We return to Mr. Domino now," Ines says.

I blink, faced with another stranger, the polar opposite to the creature I found in the mirror. It's a second before I even realize that this woman is also me. I'm as unrecognizable as before but in a very different way.

I don't dress like this—Papa would never allow it. The dress is too thin, a gauzy white material through which the dark flesh around my nipples is visible. The fabric sparkles, beaming in the harsh lighting until it hurts to stare at myself head-on.

I look away, feeling my stomach lurch as the room starts to sway beneath my feet. My eyes latch onto a nearby object that glows like a beacon, and I lurch for it. "I'm gonna be sick—"

This time I let the vomit flow freely. Before I know it, I have two of my own fingers jabbing down my tender throat to bring up more. Everything I have so that I can reset my body. Start over fresh.

Then purge again once it all feels too much.

No amount of vomit could ease the worries bearing down on me, one after the other, however. I know that. I'd have to claw out my insides to feel lighter. Rip them right out...

"Miss?" A warm hand taps my shoulder. "We return to Mr. Domino now—"

"Leave me alone!" I cling to the basin of the toilet, watching multi-colored liquid swirl in the bowl. Tan. Brown. Yellow.

I don't even know what the liquid is a remnant of. I haven't eaten. Maybe it's my soul coming up in vile-colored pieces, the last thing of value my body has left to expel.

My therapist tells me that I've been lying to myself when I claim that purging makes me feel better. Lighter, more grounded.

You're deluding yourself, Ada, she would quip. *You tell yourself that to justify the self-harm. You know what would make you feel better? Honesty. Trusting the process of therapy. Getting to the root of the issues between you and your parents. We can start with your father…*

One good thing to come out of this nightmare is that I finally have proof that all those expensive sessions were bullshit. I had the right idea all along. With emptiness comes clarity.

Finally, I can think, despite my pounding head and the fear waiting to descend the second the drug fully wears off.

Tristan is dead. My father isn't here.

I'm alone in a strange place with Domino Valenciaga.

He's protecting me, of course. From something. Those men? He hurt one of them for touching me. I remember that much, at least. But the harder I try to think, the less logical thoughts I can grasp. It's like my mind is a sieve, filtering out everything but panic and paranoia.

Something is wrong.

And my first impulse has been the one ingrained into me since childhood. Wait for orders. Papa will handle it.

He always has.

I don't know how much time passes before I finally manage to stand, leaning against the toilet for stability. For the first time, I take in my surroundings fully.

Wherever we are, it's beautiful. This bathroom is the peak of luxury with golden fixtures and the same tanned marble from the circular foyer. A long counter lines one wall, with a full-length mirror behind it, displaying my body in stark relief.

God, I look so…sickly. So weak. A shivering waif barely able to stand on her own. As I turn to inspect the rest of the room, I realize that Ines is gone. Her insistence on a particular timeline rings in my ears like an ominous warning.

Mr. Domino said ten minutes.

Mr. Domino… I never knew he had his own house, let alone his own staff. I don't even know how much he made working for my family. Could he afford a place like this on his salary? My father paid well, I'm sure. But I don't think he would pay *this* well, not even to a man whose job was to guard his secrets with his life.

More panic starts to creep in as my memories return in full. Those men brought me here for a reason. *Take his share,* Domino told one of them. His share of what?

I push those thoughts out of my head and focus on returning to the sink. I wet my fingers and work them through my hair, trying to scrub away the dry blood there. I discover a scratch, but nothing deep enough to scar—one small consolation.

I'm shallow enough to sigh in relief. For now, I'm still Ada Pavalos, blessed with the face my father staked his entire reputation on. How could a man with such a beautiful, loving family be capable of any of the atrocities the rumors circling around the city claimed?

He's an intelligent man, but his greatest asset was always his ability to subvert expectations. No one would ever expect that Roy Pavalos, with his genuine, charming grin, would ever be capable of any of the things he stood accused of.

An impending indictment would have robbed him of that trick for good. The world would have seen firsthand the evil a man like him could sow, murder being the least of his crimes. But does that make me any better?

Willing or not, I was still always an accomplice.

CHAPTER THREE

My hands are shaking when I finally finish smoothing my hair and step back from the counter. A sudden rational thought takes hold, but I gladly let it spur me into the hall, scanning wildly for Domino.

He's here to take me home, of course. Enemies of my father attacked the restaurant and killed Tristan, but Papa handled it. Domino rescued me—just as he has before. All is well.

"This way."

The voice comes from behind me, at the end of a darkened hallway. The light from the next room fills a round archway where Ines stands, her hands obediently clasped before her. She beckons me with a wave of her hand, and I find myself reentering that spacious foyer. At least four archways are leading off of it, though I can't even begin to guess to where.

It's cold in here, the kind of chill that seeps into your bones, turning every sensation into painful stimuli. The thin dress feels like weighted steel, with sharpened edges that bite at my thighs with every step I take. The neckline is far lower than I'm used to, displaying my body for whoever is near.

In this case, a pair of hungry dark eyes that take me in from across the room Ines leads me into next. It's a dining room, I think. One far larger than the one at my father's home, adorned with a rectangular glass table so long it nearly severs the room in two. The room itself is square in shape, with more round archways opening onto what looks like an open-air terrace enclosed by a wrought-iron balcony. The sky beyond it is dark, viewed from behind a row of potted palm trees that sway in a gentle breeze. Warm air blows in from outside, displacing some of that unsettling chill. I sniff, noting it's tinged with the hint of smoke. Barbecue?

I can't see any flames or a grill from here, at least.

Domino sits at the head of the table, his hands folded neatly over the glass surface. Or at least, this man sounds like my father's trusted bodyguard.

It could be my altered mental state, but he looks different. His hair is glossier than I remember, hanging loose around his shoulders, but slicked back. His skin gleams, and as I take in his outfit, I realize that it alone might be the cause for why he seems so strange.

The black silk button-up hugs the contours of his chest— and the fact that the first two are undone exposes more of him than I've ever been privy to. He doesn't ascribe to the same grueling waxing schedule as Tristan. Dark hair grows unbidden across his pecs, adding definition to the hard, rigid mounds of muscle that compose it.

For the past five years, I've only ever seen him in the same denim shirt with a collar that stretched to his neck, a straw cowboy hat, faded jeans, and the scarred leather sheath that housed his blade.

It was a memorable costume, so striking in contrast to my father's expensive tailored suits and coifed hairstyles. Roy Pavalos would never be caught dead in anything more casual than slacks. The clothing, in addition to the perfect family, only added to his persona as a seemingly honorable politician. Even his eccentric bodyguard didn't quite fit the narrative of the ruthless killers other men of power were known to keep on a leash.

I always wondered if my father was the one who insisted on the attire in the first place. It would have reinforced the illusion that this gruff, somewhat rugged foreigner must have been some cherished family friend or acquaintance that Roy Pavalos kept employed out of the goodness of his heart.

I don't get that image now. A simple change of clothing strips Domino Valenciaga of what little disarming charm he had. In its absence, the man is all darkness. Rippling muscle and terrifying strength.

My vision blurs, and I have to blink rapidly just to keep his face in focus. I don't know if I imagine the coldness in the way he looks at me, or if it's merely what his careful mask has obscured all along. Blatant, disinterest.

"Thank you, Ines," he says, waving one of his hands. "Please have Cook prepare to serve the meal we discussed. Then you can retire without any concern. *Gracias.*"

"Yes, sir." The woman nods and scurries off. My last glimpse of her expression unsettles me for reasons I can't name. She looks so…relieved.

"Where is Papa?" The question rips from me before I even fully turn back to him.

He gestures toward a chair on his left. "Have a seat, Ada."

I bristle at the authority lacing his tone. "I asked you a question—"

"You've already strained my goodwill once," he says over me. His smile is so disarming that it's nearly a full second before the ominous nature of his tone sinks in.

Strained my goodwill…

"Have a seat."

I'm too tired to argue. It's an embarrassing dance of wooden limbs and wavering balance as I stagger to the nearest chair, at least four down from the one he specified.

"Where is Papa? What… What is going on, Domino—"

"No longer will you have the right to use that name so flippantly."

My ears ring. I shake my head and blink to make sure I didn't imagine the startlingly deep baritone.

"What—"

"Your father is dead," he says. "As is your mother, though that was not my choice. Your boyfriend Tristan, as well. Your life was not spared by accident. Do you want to know my plans for you now, or after our meal?"

I rub my temples. My head is throbbing more than ever. This is all some strange hallucination. In reality, I hit my head back at the restaurant, and I'm still unconscious. A better explanation is that I never left the house. I'm in my bathroom, crouched in the corner by the sink with powder on my nose, partaking in the one act everyone always assumed was beneath me now. A year of therapy should have been the magic cure for any of my naughty habits.

But even the finest grade of coke couldn't produce a high this vivid. Gone is the manic euphoria I usually feel. Fear is a constant undercurrent, building and building at the back of my mind as if waiting for some grand moment to finally break loose.

Dead, he said. My parents. I try to process that in a dozen different ways, but none of them have the impact they should. I should be crying, I think. Gutted. Or horrified. Terrified.

It's like my body is too exhausted to go through the motions. The only coherent thought I have is that if they're truly gone...

Then no longer do I have to watch my mother waste away in silence. No longer do I have to submit myself to the will and tyranny of Roy Pavalos.

Not that the man currently in control of my life is any better.

Domino must say something else because he tilts his head expectantly. "Perhaps they gave you too strong a dose," he murmurs, and I shiver at the way his tone barely shifts. "I had them calculate the measurements with your drug history in mind."

Drug history. The way he says those two words sends my heart racing. My thoughts clear a little more as the fear grows into outright terror.

"Where am I? Where is Papa?"

"We can answer those questions all in good time," Domino says. "I will admit that I wanted to draw out this moment. Extend it for as long as possible before I told you everything. For my own selfish amusement, I wanted that. Alas, you saw more than I intended, so part of the mystery has been spoiled."

More than I intended…

"Tristan?" I croak. "What happened?"

Though I already know exactly what. He's dead.

Domino snaps his fingers, and another figure enters the room, someone taller than Ines. A man who sets a tray onto the table. It contains a bottle of wine and two glass flutes.

"My favorite vintage," Domino says once the man retreats. He grabs the bottle, reading the label. "The perfect drink to celebrate this occasion. Though, you may prefer water—" He snaps his fingers again, and the man returns with a glass pitcher of clear liquid. He pours some into one of the glasses and offers it to me. "Allow me to propose a toast. To the future, Ada-Maria. May we all receive that which we deserve."

A quiver shoots through my belly. I feel more dazed than ever. Like thinking at all requires the same effort as trudging through quicksand. Still, I try, straining to focus.

"Take it." He moved. Without my realizing it, he stood, glass in hand, and approached from my left, offering the water to me.

I reach for it and promptly spill half of the contents onto my lap. It's enormously heavy, like a lead weight in my grasp.

Unconcerned, Domino has already reclaimed his chair and began to pour himself a serving of wine.

"To new beginnings," he says, inclining his head toward me. He's drained half of his glass in a single swig by the time he cuts his gaze toward me. A glimpse of real emotion disrupts that blank, callous mask—anger. "You should drink," he warns, keeping the rim of his own glass near his mouth. "Otherwise, it's bad luck."

My hand jerks forward before I even process the motion, and more liquid spills down my front. It's ice-cold, each drop hitting my skin with a sensation reminiscent of stabbing needles—but that isn't what has me sitting straighter, every nerve on red alert.

His eyes find me, drinking in my body with an open curiosity he never displayed before.

I know I'm beautiful. Ten years after outgrowing an ugly duckling phase, it's an admission that no longer makes me feel like a conceited bitch to proudly state. I have my mother's oval face and slender body, paired with my father's large gray eyes. My body is the one attribution that I bring to the table when it comes to the Pavalos family arsenal.

My mother had her sweet, religious devotion and prominence in the local church.

My father had his political pull and the shadowy endeavors that bring in the bulk of our fortune.

I had my sex appeal. The ability to lure men into bed with only a smile and a nicely cut blouse. It was my sole thing of value. My sole purpose.

I've spent years training myself not to flinch when men of all shapes and sizes undress my body with disgusting, searching glances. After all, it was their privilege to stare.

All on Papa's say-so, how fucked up is that? The thought is one of the many dangerous ones that only creep in when I'm too high to keep them at bay. My therapist tried to insinuate that might have been one reason I found it so hard to stay clean.

Your entire life feels beyond your control. At least this way, some of that control is yours to harness.

I can't even control who I fuck and why—but I know, deep down in the part of me still tethered to some semblance of logic, that Domino never looked at me with anything remotely close to lust.

It was one of the reasons he unsettled me. One of the reasons why I'd obsess over him. When a man looked at my tits, I could gain his attention and use it to my advantage.

Domino only ever looked into my eyes with a deliberate focus. As if, to him, I was never worthy of anything more than a passing acquaintance. I always assumed it was a result of his loyalty to my father, that he didn't sexualize me out of respect.

Now, I realize just how damn naïve I'd been.

Without Papa here, those dark eyes dissect my body mercilessly, honing in on my tits and the hardened nipples protruding because of the cold. He inspects every inch of me he can without being hindered by the table. By the time I remember how to move, he's already taking another sip of his wine.

"We have much to discuss, Ada-Maria," he says. "I think our meal might be ready."

This time, he claps his hands together, summoning a train of four people who stream into the room from the direction of the terrace, each holding a different platter of food. The smells are dizzying, triggering another wave of nausea. The fact that my stomach is empty might be the only reason why I don't vomit again.

One by one, the different dishes adorn the table, each more complex than the last. Fresh rolls. A salad. An array of fruit. A plate of roasted meat appears to be the crowning dish.

My mother couldn't have done better.

The smells churn my stomach.

"This meal is in your honor, Ada-Maria. I hope everything is to your liking." Domino waves his hand, cueing one of the servers to cut the roast, while another sets about compiling two plates with equal helpings of the various dishes.

They place one in front of me.

"Eat," Domino says.

I've spent enough time around men in power to know an order when I hear one. Unfortunately for him, this is one realm in which I've always had control over. Not even my father could take that tiny shred of power from me. Aware of him watching, I clamp my lips together.

"I said *eat*."

His voice… It sounds like the man I've always known to cling to my father's coattails, but with subtle changes. Like a familiar song played backward, and the once unthreatening melody takes on an unsettling tempo.

"Did you hear me, Ada-Maria?"

I push the plate aside. Or I try to. I'm too weak to make it move more than a few inches, but the impression is the same regardless.

"Where is Papa?"

He cocks his head and swipes his thumb across his lower lip. "You should eat."

"I'm not hungry," I lie. My words slur, my pitch wavering. "What the hell is going on—"

"Eat."

"Who the hell do you think you are to speak to me like this?"

The latter half of that statement is still on my tongue—*I am a Pavalos!* The magic phrase that has been able to cow anyone from childhood bullies to government officials. The only worth my life seems to hold these days.

But his voice overpowers me before I can even utter it. "I've humored your disobedience once," he says. "You already owe repentance for being twenty-two minutes late—despite poor Ines' best efforts to remind you of our engagement. Don't make me add rudeness onto your impending punishment, Ada-Maria."

The air escapes my lungs, squeezed out by how violently my chest contracts.

Roy Pavalos had a beautiful, playful cadence that could turn any compliment into a song of the highest praise. At least when he wanted to.

Otherwise, he could stop the devil himself in his tracks with one word alone. My father, the power player. The admirable politician. The brutal crime lord.

I've never known anyone capable of rivaling the power he could command through his voice.

Until now.

I don't recognize this man. That familiar face takes on a newer entity—that of a dangerous figure I'm ill-equipped to face alone.

Where is Papa?

"For the last time, I'm telling you to eat."

I snatch a fork and stab it into the nearest item on my plate —a few leaves of a garden salad. I shove them into my mouth and chew, tasting nothing but salt. Blood.

A gag contorts my throat before I can help it, and green-colored liquid spills onto the table's polished surface.

"Try the au gratin potatoes," Domino says. I notice that he doesn't touch his own food.

I shake my head, my stomach heaving. "I'm not hungry—"

"I see you've made your choice." He smiles in a startling display of white teeth. Against his skin, they seem to glow. "Let's take a walk on the terrace, shall we?"

He stands. Three strides bring him to my side before I even finish processing his suggestion. His hand lands on my shoulder, and my entire body goes numb. I've had to endure so many different kinds of touch in my life. Wanted. Unwanted. Reviled.

He inspires so many reactions at once my body overloads on them.

"Join me, Ada-Maria." His voice sounds deeper than before, sinking into my muscle and bone like a wrench that physically yanks me to my feet. My head swims as I find myself staggering in his wake. Around the massive table. Through one of the archways into the warm night air that completely displaces any remaining chill, slicking my skin with a sheen of sweat.

The scent of barbecue grows stronger. Potent. Pork, I think…

Though it's been so damn long since I've imbibed anything more than lettuce and boiled eggs. And crusty restaurant bread.

"You didn't try the meat," Domino admonishes. His voice seems to carry further out here—a wide, circular balcony overlooking a bubbling fountain set within a square pool illuminated with delicate orange lanterns. A private garden, but not the one on my father's estate—or any that I know of for that matter.

"Where are we?"

"My cook will be insulted, Ada-Maria," he says as if I never spoke. Why? I struggle to follow the conversation. Something about the meat. "He prepared it just for you. It took him days to research the recipe best able to make such an exotic protein palatable. I'm disappointed."

We round the curve, and more of the terrace comes into view—an even wider section with white couches arranged around a fire pit. The stench of burning and smoke is suddenly stronger, irritating my eyes.

As they water, I spot the source of the smell—the meat is cooking here on a spit set above the flames. It's large. A cow? Or maybe a pig, set far enough back from the flames themselves that the meat blisters and crackles from the heat, but isn't burned. But wait…

"He hasn't come up with a name for this new dish yet," Domino continues. He releases me and approaches the spit, inspecting the cooking meat.

Something about it keeps drawing my notice. The shape isn't right… The proportions are far too slender to belong to any pig I've ever seen. Science was never my forte, and my education doesn't extend beyond high school. I'm no expert on biology—but I do know the human body. Men, to be exact.

The way they carry muscle. How their limbs can contort and how foreign they can appear when limp and flaccid.

Blood rushes to my head, deafening me to anything else he might say. Not only is the shape of this "animal" unusual, but the skin…

It's darker in places and nearly stark white in others. Like clothing?

Slowly, my gaze roves to Domino, and I find him watching me. The orange glow of the blaze reflects off his eyes. My suspicion wasn't wrong. He is the devil, gloating mercilessly as realization dawns over me with a horrifying certainty.

That is not a pig.

Domino's lips part, and I hear his voice again. *Only* him, as if this low, callous baritone is meant just for me. "I've suggested *Pollo de Roy*. It has a rather literal meaning, but I think it gets the point across."

Spanish was one of the few bits of study my father instilled in me, though I'm nowhere near fluent. I have to parse through the words as my eyes return to the spit. *Pollo*, chicken. Except this creature is far too large to be that of one small bird. *De*, means of. The last word I can't make sense of.

Roy…

A flicker of material catches my interest as the spit slowly turns. Fabric? It's slender, dancing in the breeze. At one point, it might have been a light blue despite parts of it blackening by the proximity to the flames.

My father's signature color. He always claimed it complemented his gray eyes, identical to mine. They were one of the few things we actually shared. Our eyes. Our tempers. Our penchant for sinning mercilessly to get what we wanted.

"I wish you could have sampled a taste, Ada-Maria," Domino says, his tone richer than ever, as if he's on the verge of laughter. "I've heard the flavor compared to chicken, but I'm inclined to describe this particular protein as tasting more like the finest fat, suckling pig."

Blackness. When my vision returns, I'm on my knees, tasting salt and earth. The once peaceful terrace is now ablaze with grating, loud noise. A keening cry-like sound that pierces my eardrums. I want it to stop.

It's only as my throat aches with my next intake of air that I realize the sound is coming from me.

Screaming.

Endless screaming.

CHAPTER FOUR

"Mr. Domino requests you in twenty minutes." The persistent, soft murmur draws me from a sleep too heavy to feel natural.

My body is a mass of varying aches and pains, each one blaring for attention the second I peel my eyes open to a mockingly bright ceiling.

Clara is my usual maid, but she knows better than to wake me up unceremoniously—unless Papa demands it, of course. Usually, by that point, I'm already late. What party or function am I doomed to be tardy for today?

Groaning, I roll onto my side, still processing her words. *Mr. Domino.* I stop dead, registering that name at the exact moment that I realize this room isn't my own.

The walls are white, the floor a familiar tan marble that seems to be the signature sight of this unending nightmare. The bed beneath me is larger than mine, the sheets the same shade as the walls.

The room itself is spacious, with a row of curved French-style windows—each one shrouded in lacy white curtains—letting in golden sunlight from the left.

At the foot of the bed stands a woman I vaguely recognize, her graying hair pulled tight into a bun.

"Mr. Domino requests you in twenty minutes," she insists. With a wave of her hand, she gestures to a metal clothing rack beside her. A single dress hangs from it—a frothy white wisp of lace and gauzy material that looks thin enough to rip should I attempt to put it on.

At the base of the rack is a pair of delicate white heels.

Neither garment is anything remotely close to what I own.

Because I'm not at home. My head is throbbing, filtering thoughts stupidly slow. The memories from last night are scattered snippets, but a part of me instinctively shies from inspecting them. *Not now.*

Instead, I focus on taking stock of my body as I sit upright and push the sheets aside.

The mattress is surprisingly soft—therefore not the source of the pain shooting through my lower back and my hip. Wincing, I crane my neck to inspect the area and find myself having to yank up the hem of another thin white dress.

It's similar to the one awaiting me, though shorter. The material, however, is fine enough to see the mottled bruising forming over my upper thigh, before I even yank the fabric away. That's not all. Small scrapes and cuts speckle my arms and legs, and my head feels so tender that even breathing hurts.

"Please, Miss," Ines calls. Something in her tone has me scooting to the edge of the mattress, despite the discomfort. Fear?

She doesn't meet my gaze long enough for me to be sure. Instead, she guides me into sitting on the edge of the mattress and tugs the dress I'm wearing over my head.

Within less than a minute, I'm wearing the fresh clothing, and she's urging me across the room to stand before a full-length mirror.

"Wait, please." She scurries off through a door while I face myself.

I feel so disconnected from the body before me. Only those familiar gray eyes trigger any semblance of recognition, though the whites surrounding them are bloodshot. A dark bruise paints the flesh above my right temple, centered around a scabbed-over gash.

Overall, it's the dress that I find the hardest to stomach. It's too pretty. Too sexy—a constant reminder of the dangerous reality lurking at the back of my mind. Something is wrong.

Domino.

He isn't in this room now, nor is he visible beyond the doorway as Ines returns, a silver tray in hand.

"Mr. Domino insists," she explains almost apologetically. I don't understand her hesitancy. At first glance, the tray holds nothing overly menacing, just a matching silver brush and comb, a small glass bottle of amber liquid, and…

"No—" The word slips from my throat as I step back, shaking my head. Panic is an animal clawing through my chest, threatening to unleash the full weight of all the memories I've kept at bay until now.

"Please, Miss. Mr. Domino insists," Ines warns. Again, something in her tone reaches through my building terror despite every cell in my body urging me to run.

If I had any hope that my recollections were all a nightmare, this new development alone proves me wrong.

No hero would insist on the woman he saved wearing what lies on that tray. Only a monster.

"Please, Miss. We have five minutes," Ines says, her voice wavering.

I don't move as she sets the tray on a nearby white dresser, carved with ornate reliefs of crawling vines and round fruit that resemble oranges. She lifts the brush and comb first, using them in tandem to tackle my hair. Then she dabs drops of the liquid over my neck. Perfume, I realize as the smell tickles my nostrils.

It's light and crisp, also reminiscent of oranges.

Finally, Ines lifts the final object and approaches me slowly, as if giving me ample time to resist. When I don't, she secures the item around my neck with a brisk familiarity that makes me suspect this isn't the first time she's done so.

On how many women? Did they all wake up in this same white room?

Were they all served pieces of their own father?

No. I squeeze my eyes shut, blocking out the images. I can't focus on them; I can't. Ironically, it's the same mindset my father himself taught me. Focus only on the present. What matters. Survival.

Ignore the rest. Don't dwell on what may or may not be— only the present.

You are a Pavalos.

"We have two minutes." The quiet voice intrudes on the monologue, but I welcome the distraction.

When I open my eyes again, I detach myself from the woman displayed on the glass before me and objectively inspect the item around her throat. It's well-crafted enough to pass as some beautiful fashion accessory—not a collar.

It's about an inch wide, formed of polished white leather, with a golden clasp responsible for the subtle weight I feel against my throat. One detail that separates it from an innocent necklace, however, is the distinct indent in the center of the golden clasp—a keyhole. A few inches down from it, is a golden ring embedded in the leather, protruding slightly. The perfect attachment for a leash.

I've seen dog collars more subtle.

My eyelids flutter helplessly as moisture forms beneath them, burning and searing, blurring my vision. I barely see Ines' face as she takes one of my hands, urging me after her. She's a blob of color against this otherwise stark white realm.

I follow her blindly, shocked when we appear in another room as if teleported there. I think I recognize it. A large circular foyer bathed in sunlight, with windows and doorways arching from it; the same place I woke up in last night.

"Morning, Ada-Maria." This iteration of Domino Valenciaga is still almost unrecognizable, dressed in black, the top buttons of his shirt undone. He sits before a small round table set for two and beckons me closer with a wave of his hand. "Thank you, Ines."

From the corner of my eye, I see the woman rush from the room, leaving us alone.

I'm tired enough to assume that the figure before me couldn't possibly be the man I've spent five years near. They don't even carry themselves the same. The Domino who served my father did so quietly in the background, his posture such that, even with his bulk, he could seamlessly blend into the scenery when necessary.

And, during the moments my father needed to make a point, the man could serve as a menacing, unmistakable presence.

"You…" My throat is so dry it hurts to speak louder than a whisper. Even then, I have to battle with the chirping of nearby birds and the rustling of the wind through the room's linen curtains to be heard. "You killed Papa—"

"Bygones," Domino says forcefully with another wave. His lips form an expression far too emotionless to be called a smile. It's merely the shadow of one. "I suggest you focus on preserving your own life, Ada-Maria."

Fear and exhaustion go to war over what little part of my mind is functional enough to think logically.

Focus, Papa would say. *Ignore the emotion. You are a Pavalos, not some sniveling whore. Act like it.*

"Have a seat." Again, Domino waves toward the chair across from him, but I don't move.

"Where am I?"

Not in Terra Rodea. I can't quite explain why, but the air tastes different than it does in the heart of the city. We must be somewhere beyond it. The countryside? Far from the city limits to justify the expansive gardens I remember from last night.

In the light of day, the architecture of this room alone is blatantly opulent. Though minimal, I can tell this property is expensive. A house perhaps, in the style of the older villas like the kind my uncle Rodrigo owns in Mexico. Regardless, it's somewhere that even the best-paid bodyguard would have trouble affording.

In fact, anyone who could purchase such an estate wouldn't need to work a menial job at all.

Seconds tick by as I realize he deliberately left my question unanswered. His eyes rake over my body, and I'm painfully reminded of how thin this dress is. I wasn't supplied any underwear, and the warm breeze blowing in ruffles the short hemline, snatching it from my body in a way that risks exposing what little the material does cover. All I can do is press it flat with both hands.

A rich, deep laugh rings out, startling me so badly I nearly lose my grip in shock.

"Please, Ada-Maria. The longer you delay with pointless questions, the more you prolong our much overdue discussion. You know where you are," he declares, his eyes narrowing. "The gist of it, anyway. Somewhere far beyond your father's influence. So, I suggest you drop the sheltered princess routine and act accordingly."

Something in his tone spurs me forward. I'm shaking, my knees knocking together with every step I take. When I grip the back of the chair to pull it out, I nearly tip it over.

A tanned hand shoots out, gripping the wooden frame just inches from where mine rests.

"Allow me." He stands, triggering a rush of cologne and musk to hit my nose in a battering wave. Did he always smell like this? Intoxicating, but in a bad way. Too many nuanced scents to make sense of all at once. My brain aches with the effort, and I'm caught off guard when he appears directly behind me.

"Sit." The heat of his breath is scalding, raising sweat that instantly glues the thin layer of fabric to my skin.

I obey—my knees bending to drop me on the edge of the chair—more out of a need to put any amount of distance between us that I can.

My heartbeat plays an unsettling melody as he lingers behind me. The murmuring nature isn't loud enough to drown out the ragged sound of his inhale. Alarm shoots through me, straightening my spine.

God only knows what he wants with me, and, for the first time, I toy with the more dangerous possibilities I haven't let myself consider before. Rape. Torture. Murder.

He's made you wear a goddamn collar, Ada—

"I will tell you when it's time to fear me," Domino says, his tone casual as he reclaims his chair. He could be referring to the weather if the words alone didn't contain a thinly veiled threat. "I suggest you save your energy for when that moment comes. In the meantime, relax. I've had Ines prepare some tea."

As he speaks, I notice the white porcelain teapot resting before him, pale enough to blend in with the table's ivory surface. An exotic scent emanates from it, tickling my nose. It's unlike any tea I've ever smelled.

Instantly, my suspicions run wild—especially considering one fact that occurs to me now. "You drugged me."

He laughs again, sitting back in his seat. While holding my gaze, he snaps his fingers, and a different woman appears from the direction of the terrace. Racing forward, she scrambles to pour the steaming liquid from the kettle into two delicate cups.

"The men I hired to apprehend you drugged you," Domino says, reaching for the nearest teacup. "Though, given your history, I'm sure it was nothing your system couldn't handle. Already, you're awake and alert. What a miracle. Another woman your size would still be unconscious."

I stiffen at the implied insult, swallowing hard. This very man must have sat across from my father all these years while he received every frantic phone call and wrote the check for every therapist or brief stint in rehab. My father didn't give a damn about my habit in general. Only to the extent that it might reflect poorly on him if I were stupid enough to be caught high in public.

But even my father wouldn't dare use my sobriety against me. The full extent of the danger facing me sinks in like a gut punch. This man is no stranger. He's seen me at my lowest throughout the years and watched my father navigate some of the most challenging moments in my life. He knows the Pavalos family in and out.

And he betrayed us.

"Drink, Ada-Maria," he says before sipping from his own cup.

I eye my hand, pale and limp, against the table's surface. In slow motion, I watch those fingers twitch to life, and every digit extend outward. Then I bat the teacup and send it flying, spraying boiling liquid in an arch.

It falls short, landing inches from my feet. Stray drops speckle my thigh, and I flinch at the searing pain.

And yet, the effect is clear—defiance.

"You will pay for that." Domino barely pauses before taking his next sip to utter the threat, but I feel it resonate down to my very core.

The way his voice vibrates through flesh and bone seems to shake a million different revelations loose all at once. Primarily one.

Run, Ada!

I jerk to my feet, pushing the chair over in my haste. I don't know which doorway leads to an exit. I pick the direction of the terrace, racing out into the blinding sun.

The beauty I find is such a stark contrast to the fear building in my veins. As every atrocity I've witnessed flashes through my mind, it's like my surroundings become even more dreamlike to counter the brutality.

It's as if the world itself is mocking me.

The morbid images of Tristan's death don't match with the beautiful blue sky visible from a swath of swaying palm trees and potted ferns. The horror of being drugged clashes with the bountiful gardens that seem to go on forever beyond this balcony.

The casual setting of white lounge chairs around a pristine fire pit doesn't seem capable of holding the smoldering remains of a human body.

My father…

I sway and trip, landing hard on my right knee, tasting blood on my tongue. The sunlight lances through my skull every time I blink, my brain on fire, the noise of birds and insects swelling to a buzzing drone that grows louder and louder…

I'm suffocating.

"I didn't want to use this unless absolutely necessary." Like ice, that voice banishes all else in its wake. The world goes dead silent as a shadow falls over me, dark enough to obscure all traces of sunlight.

The devil looms above, his eyes ablaze. They aren't completely dark, I realize. I've never been close enough to make out the subtle green lurking beneath the swaths of brown before. A hellish hazel.

Much like this property, he's too beautiful to seem capable of sowing the fear that breaks loose, constricting my chest and flooding my eyes with tears.

I can't breathe. Can't think.

I can only stare as he reaches for my throat and his thick fingers snag the thin leather of my collar.

He's choking me…

Abruptly, he lets go. Something swings between us as he steps back, and it takes my brain almost a full second to name it. A thin golden chain that feels surprisingly heavy. One end is looped around his fist, and the other…

He tugs, and my body jerks forward, forcing me to brace my weight over my hands. I gag as the pressure around my throat tightens. With one hand, I reach up, feeling along the leather until my fingers strike the once inexplicable ring of gold. Only now it's not empty—he's attached the other end of the chain to it.

Like a leash.

"On your feet," he demands.

The pressure returns, tight enough to crush my throat. My body moves automatically to lessen the discomfort, and I stagger to my feet, my eyes watering.

He's cruel, stalking ahead at a seemingly leisurely pace that I have to lurch to keep up with. I realize, horrified, that he isn't heading inside.

From my peripheral vision, I see other people lurking in the fields or passing beyond the archways inside the house. Servants? None seem alarmed by the man dragging me to the edge of the balcony.

"Take it in, Ada-Maria. Would you like to guess where we are?"

I sense that he doesn't require an answer.

Regardless, I blink, struggling to make sense of the fields in a different context from their sheer beauty. It's warmer here than it should be this time of year. The foreign scent in the air is more potent now.

I can't even begin to guess where we are.

"I wanted to draw out this moment, I will admit," Domino explains, winding the chain around his fist, forcing me closer. Closer. My feet wobble in these heels, threatening my precarious balance.

Suddenly, I'm thrown forward, forced to grapple for the railing to keep from flying over it. I taste my pulse as I eye the stone courtyard awaiting below.

"It is a beautiful view," Domino says. "This home has been in my family for generations. The land, at least. I'm surprised you don't remember it."

Remember?

He's insane—or worse, he's toying with me, playing with word games and riddles. Irritation combats the fear just long enough for me to choke out a reply.

"You were a guard."

He laughs at the insinuation.

"I was a *guard*," he echoes, his voice booming. "How the hell could I afford so much as a stone? It's how your father taught you to see the world. In numbers and worth. In your limited thinking, someone like me could never amass a fortune of his own. Only on the back of men like Don Roy."

I tremble at the title. How soon have I forgotten what he called my father day in and day out. *Don Roy.* Typically, he uttered it with a quiet reverence that always irritated me for reasons I can't explain.

Everyone spoke of my father the same way. Like he was God. A man so righteous he commanded respect from even his enemies.

I used to wonder if they were that desperate for a paycheck to grovel before him or just *that* blinded by money and power. They thought those fragile symbols of power made a man invincible.

Now, I sense it was all an act—at least where Domino Valenciaga is concerned. He never respected my father. Otherwise, he wouldn't be able to say his name with such disdain.

I don't know why that realization startles me so damn much.

My therapist claimed my drug use stemmed from a lack of control in my life. I would describe it more like exhaustion. I became so damn tired of playing my role like the perfect daughter worthy of the magnanimous Roy Pavalos. I always suspected that everyone around me was doing the same, merely going through the motions like automatons at one of those arcade-style restaurants my parents took me to as a child. We all sing and dance and play by the rules provided to us, knowing that everyone else is in on the show. It's all smoke and mirrors, but we'd die to keep the performance running smoothly.

It's another thing entirely to watch someone willfully drop the façade, exposing just how fake it all truly is, how false my life has always been.

A game. A lie. A twisted play.

A routine I have no idea how to survive outside of.

CHAPTER FIVE

"H-How?" I croak, craning my neck to face him. His grip on the leash keeps me hunched over. From this angle, I can only see his profile, stern and emotionless.

"How could I afford this?" He gestures with a wave of his free hand to the gardens. They extend as far as the eye can see. "Or how could I slip under your father's radar for so long? Don't play coy, Ada-Maria. Ignorance doesn't suit you. In fact, I'll humor your questions, so ask them while you can."

I suck in a breath. I'm shivering, my teeth chattering despite the sweat I can feel beading over the back of my neck. It's swelteringly hot in the direct sun.

"Where are we?"

"That question I won't answer just yet," he says with a laugh.

The chain flashes in the light as he manipulates it so that I'm fully upright, no longer leaning over the railing.

"Try another."

"My father…" The rest of the words die in my throat. I don't expect the tears that fall, blinding me to everything else. Wracking sobs rip from my chest, and I welcome them. I don't care if it's a display of weakness. At least I can't hear. I can't think.

As long as I give into the fear, I'm unaware of anything else.

Until my windpipe is being crushed by the pressure of the collar. I'm on my knees, gasping for air. I'm choking…

I'm dying…

"Look at me."

I sputter as the pressure loosens enough for me to look up into the impassive face of the man before me. He's crouched on one knee, the chain wound almost entirely around his fist.

"I won't tolerate your fear," he tells me. "Your sniveling attempts at innocence. I am not one of your many, *many* paramours, Ada-Maria. When you speak to me, you speak with conviction. No games. Understood?"

The chain clatters as he loosens his grasp, letting nearly the entire length pool on the courtyard between us.

I flinch back, bracing my hands against the stone beneath me. This dress is too small, bunched around my thighs, the neckline gaping below my chest enough for him to see everything at a glance.

I bolt upright onto my knees, grappling to cover my exposed breasts.

He laughs in a way that makes me feel completely naked. Stripped. Every low chuckle creeps beneath this gauzy fabric in a way his eyes—or his hands—never could.

"What did you really mean to ask me?" he prods.

I rub my throat until I catch my breath again. "You killed my father." It feels so strange to admit. A part of me doesn't believe it.

Someone like Roy Pavalos can't just *die.* He can't wind up turning on a spit over an open fire.

He was larger than life, a creature I always assumed was too big to ever fall. Even a jail sentence wouldn't stop him for long.

"There now," Domino growls, his eyes gleaming. "Continue."

I lick my lips to gain enough traction to croak a single word. "Why?"

"Why gut your father like a pig?" He smiles, and I recoil, feeling my heart hammer against my ribcage. It's not the expression alone that inspires the reaction—objectively, it's a beautiful grin, enhancing the strange greenish hue to his eyes—but what alarms me is the fact that it's real. He's enjoying this. "I'm sure you can think of several reasons. I want you to pick one, Ada-Maria."

I manipulate my tongue to reply. "He trusted you."

And he did, allowing his virtual shadow to accompany him everywhere. At his office. Family gatherings. His political meetings. There wasn't a place Roy Pavalos went without his trusty protector Domino.

Part of the reason was that, as a man in his position, his life was always in danger. But there was another explanation, one my father would boast about on any occasion where he happened to drink too much wine. Smiling with pride, he'd discuss the origin of how he met his valuable friend and asset. Hell, I think he staked part of his political campaign on it.

Roy Pavalos, *el Salvador*.

The savior of all.

"He saved you—"

Stars explode to life before me, rivaling the intensity of the sun. My ears are ringing, my tongue flooded with the taste of salt. When I gasp in shock, I realize why. My mouth is on fire. Throbbing. Bleeding…

And Domino's fist is raised, his eyes so dark they suck all the warmth from the world itself, like smoldering coals feeding on anything remotely peaceful. He is hell incarnate.

"I knew you were a dumb cunt, Ada-Maria, but I didn't believe that you were ever *that* goddamn foolish."

He's already storming toward another part of the terrace. Belatedly, I realize that the chain is still in his grasp. I watch the pool of gold on the paving stones unravel, growing smaller and smaller until…

I'm tugged forward, forced to scramble to my feet to keep my airway clear. The ability to breathe is a luxury he makes me chase him for. Eyes streaming, throat burning, I nearly gasp in relief as he finally comes to a stop before an area I recognize with chilling familiarity.

"Your father didn't rescue me from some *barrio* with the promise of cash and freedom in America, Ada-Maria. Do you want to hear how we really met?"

His hand swings out, shoving me onto the nearest couch. I fall back, nearly sliding off the surface entirely. Panicked, I realize that my dress rode up my hips as a result, exposing everything from the waist down. I snatch at the hem, yanking it into place, not that he seems to notice.

Or care.

That piercing gaze is fixated in the distance. In the past, I suspect, far beyond me.

"That bastard got himself in deep with a particular cartel," he murmurs. "One of the many he toyed with. They sent an assassin to cut off his dick and return it to the boss on a silver platter. Until someone took the liberty of cutting off the bastard's head and rescuing dear old Don Roy from certain death."

He cuts his gaze to me expectantly, and the chain rattles against the stones like a drumroll to herald the question he deliberately left for me to answer.

"Y-You?"

He nods. "*Sí*. I rescued that crooked motherfucker, and he welcomed me back with open arms. Hell, he practically begged me to ensure his safe passage back to his dear wife and loving daughter. I hadn't planned on that, you see. I didn't expect worming my way into his life would be that damn easy."

I flinch. It's such a callous admission. He sought out my father. Earned his trust. For five years, he worked for him diligently without a word of complaint, as far as I knew.

"Why?"

He laughs again, raising the hair on the back of my neck. "Why? Because the best revenge, dear Ada-Maria, is done slowly, over time, so that it ripens nice and sweet. Slowly enough so that when the time came, and I finally looked that bastard in the eye as my true self, all would become clear. How blind he was all along. How he trusted his wife and whore of a daughter to a snake. For a man who prided himself so damn much on his honor and his vigilance, he didn't even realize that the man he entrusted his life to had introduced his precious daughter to cocaine, and ensured that his wife found out about every little dalliance and indiscretion. Every cheap, desperate secretary or intern that he'd fuck in the cabana on the estate. Don't look so surprised, Ada-Maria," he scolds, eyeing me from over his shoulder. "Don't tell me you believed yourself the tragic little heroine of your own fucked-up fairy tale? No. God himself isn't anywhere near as malicious as I am."

The worst part is I don't even know if he's lying or not. My mind is a blur as the past and present meld. A million little things I never inspected in full, now seem woefully important.

I took drugs at the first party I snuck into on my own. Daddy had been too absorbed by his new campaign, and I convinced myself that a small act of rebellion would secure his attention. I only wanted him to hear me, for once. To truly consider my request to study abroad—everyone else with less money and even fewer brains than I had was already pledged to some prestigious university or the other.

No one else had been destined to die in Terra Rodea because their father thought they had more use as a prop to sell his political career than as a human being with an ounce of self-determination.

My way of reclaiming a shred of that control had been to find the most dangerous man I could and let him do whatever he wanted…

As long as he gave me a little sliver of freedom to hold onto, all I had to do was shove it up my nose.

"Did you think you were so unlucky?" Domino asks, his tone mocking once more. "You were always a pawn. Though I will give you some credit—you were never as easy to predict as your father. Don Roy was a smart motherfucker."

A genuine hint of admiration in his voice breaks through the hate.

"It took effort to outsmart him. Years of patience, and research, and waiting. But you? You were like a fucking rabbit born without an ounce of self-preservation. So desperate. So weak. At every turn, I found myself overestimating your sheer stupidity."

"What did you want?"

The way his eyes slice through me reveals a hint of irritation he usually conceals. As he clenches his jaw, I think I know why—I had the nerve to interrupt him.

Hiss. The sound of the chain plays like an ominous soundtrack—a constant reminder of the power he holds in this situation. The ability to choke me should he choose to.

To kill me.

And yet, I sense that I've contradicted his very statement. I've unnerved him.

So, I keep talking. "Why pretend? Why play the puppet master. Why kill…"

I still can't admit out loud what my eyes—and my nose—confirmed to be true. Papa is dead. And so much of the person I've strived to be dies with him. All of the secrets I've kept. All of the lies I told. Maybe Domino Valenciaga is my punishment for all of it…

"I'm rethinking my decision to spare you." His tone is so blunt. The sheer implications of his words land a second too late. I wince, clenching my teeth together so violently they clatter.

His decision to spare me…

At the expense of someone else.

"You killed Tristan."

His death isn't as easy to doubt. I saw him. I heard the impact of his body hitting the floor. I tasted his blood and felt the heat of it bathe my skin. I saw the bloodied socket where his head used to be.

"You're a monster. You're sick. You're—"

Cling! The musical chime echoes as he whips his arm through the air, gathering up another loop of the chain. Due to the shortened length, I'm pulled upright, forced to sit on the edge of the couch.

"There will be plenty of time for hysterics later," he says, his tone devoid of anything but ice. "You want to prolong your pathetic, worthless life, Ada-Maria? Then it's time for me to ask the questions. Just one, to make it easy for your little brain to handle—where is the file?"

I blink.

His eyes cut to slits, and the chain becomes taut between us. I gag, my eyes watering. Helpless, my hands fly to the base of the chain, tugging to lessen the pressure on my throat.

"Don't play dumb now." He takes a step, then another, winding the chain all the while until he's standing before me within arm's reach. "You may help him win the horny bachelor vote when it comes to political prospects, but you and I both know that he's kept you close all this time for more than that. Think, Ada-Maria. Where is the Inglecias file?"

Inglecias. I haven't heard that name in so long. Just that particular arrangement of syllables triggers a reaction in me —I gag, hunching over, in case there's anything left in my stomach to bring up.

There isn't.

I realize he's watching, but I'm not faking being the dumb blond for once. He's served my father long enough to know more about the Inglecias incident than I do. I barely remember it, let alone a file. Though honestly, I've spent the past decade trying to forget.

The past.

Pia.

Everything.

"Where is it?" Domino demands.

I look up, eyeing him through my tousled hair. He looks different, his head cocked expectantly, his eyes practically glowing with interest. This isn't a random request. He's desperate for it, this file on one of the vilest periods in my family's history.

My heart races with dread as to why he's interested in that particular incident, but—physical reaction aside—I don't hesitate to say, "I don't know anything about a file."

He frowns, his brows furrowing.

Cling! He jerks his fist, and I'm crashing onto the floor, dragged toward him by the force he easily applies to the collar. It hurts. Fire lances through my windpipe, and I fear that he's crushed it this way. I'll die slowly, suffocated by the damage.

Somehow, I manage to sputter down spurts of fresh air as he finally relents.

"You're lying." His voice is a chilling array of deep, resonating notes—but I'm beginning to pick up on the rare hints of emotion when they do peek through. It's easy, in a sense, given how flat he usually sounds. Anger adds color to the rich baritone. It will haunt my nightmares forever after this.

If I live…

"Pia, Navid, and Rosa Inglecias. Don't tell me your father didn't keep a record of what he did to them."

Because Roy Pavalos kept records on everything. From political rivals to the names of the lowest-ranked reporter who might be brazen enough to publish an obscure blog post about him. He knew everything about everyone.

Except, it seems, Domino Valenciaga.

"You would know," I whisper, and he raises an eyebrow, flexing his wrist.

I tense in anticipation of more pressure, but he merely tugs. Just a tease.

"One might think I would," he says softly. With his free hand, he captures his chin, stroking the dark stubble there.

Of all the times to have this thought, this is the least advantageous. It creeps in regardless, the biting, underlying truth that I always considered him attractive. Repressed, rebellious girls have repressed, rebellious thoughts. Like fantasies of seducing their father's trusted bodyguard and convincing him to steal her away. I've always consoled myself with the caveat that if I truly wanted him, I could have him. After all, I could land any man I wanted with a bat of my eyelashes and a wink.

It was a lie. No matter how many times I tried to meet his gaze in the past, Domino barely paid me any notice. And every taste of his indifference just fed my little private hunger more. There's something alluring in being ignored. Especially when the whole damn world seems to crave being inside your body. Or your head.

He never seemed to want either.

Now I know why.

"What did my father ever do to you?" I ask, my voice hoarse and broken.

"That is a tale for another day." Abruptly, he releases my chain and snaps his fingers. "Ines?"

The woman takes just seconds to appear. "Yes, sir?"

"Take Ms. Pavalos to her room. See that she bathes and rests —" His attention returns to me, his tone far more cutting. "You'll need it, Ada-Maria. Later tonight, we will discuss your transgression and how you may make amends. *Adios.*"

He walks away, leaving my chain untethered. Dazed, I stare after him, barely aware when a small figure stoops to grab the chain and gently winds it around her fingers.

"Here, Miss—" I jump as Ines appears by my side, pressing something cool against my hand. When glimpsed on my palm, it's unsettling just how small and delicate the golden chain appears. So light, I barely feel the pressure when held, and yet my throat is on fire. I can only take a few breaths at a time before needing to swallow just to relieve the burn, wincing at the sensation.

"This way," Ines calls, reaching for my hand.

I find that I can't tear my gaze from the man pacing the balcony with his back to me. I get the sense that I've confused him somehow. I've irritated him further.

Everything—from his behavior to the violence I've barely let myself relive—feels like I'm only seeing part of some elaborate puzzle. Or a game.

My father was known for them. When other men invited their guests to the strip club or lavish parties, my father hosted chest tournaments fueled by liquor and bets.

If one of you can beat me, he'd say to preface the event, *I'll give you whatever you fucking want. Anything. My house. My money. My ass.*

A harsh laugh would trigger everyone else to join in, lightening the mood despite the thrill of competition he loved to foster.

I'll let you have it all, he claimed. *You only need to beat me once.*

Suffice to say, no one ever could.

CHAPTER SIX

The second Ines leads me back to that white room; I fixate on the bed. I lunge for it. Crawling beneath the covers is a coping mechanism I've retained from childhood, but I indulge it, even now.

Buried beneath the fine, silken sheets, I feel invisible. Smothered. Silenced. If I close my eyes and slam my hands over my ears, I can almost pretend that I'm beyond this place, as insignificant as a snail buried in mud, unnoticed by all, wanted by no one.

That used to be my most fiercely wished-for dream —irrelevance.

Ines, however, is not my usual maid—who learned early on not to bother me when I'm in this state. Fearlessly, she flips back the blankets, her voice persistent enough to seep into my skull no matter how hard I press my hands against it.

"Please, Miss, Mr. Domino requested that you—"

"Please, leave me alone!" My voice echoes back to me, wild and hysterical. "Please. I just need a minute, please?" I sense her withdraw though I don't know if she ever leaves. I just burrow beneath the sheets again, wrestling with the part of me that wants to ignore, and the faint whisper of instinct warning me to get my bearings and find a way out.

The inner voice is harder to smother without drugs or alcohol. Combined, they're enough to silence that feeble thread of my conscience, but this time, it lives on, seeping through the chaos of my mind, presenting the reality I can't hide from.

Domino killed my father. He killed Tristan, and trapped me here. All for what?

Something to do with the Inglecias family.

It's funny how you can spend nearly every day in someone's orbit. For that fragment of time, they become the center of your universe. You know everything about them. You've tailored your entire life to reacting to their voice. Their smell. Their laughter.

And then one day, they're just gone, leaving no choice but to cope with their absence—but it's hard. Like adjusting to life with an amputated limb. Only you have no idea how or why it went missing in the first place.

Pia Inglecias was my best friend. We did everything together. We shared secrets, clothes, and even our beds, spending nearly every night in my room or hers. She was one of the few people my father ever allowed into his coveted world.

Until she vanished without a trace, and I went from talking to her every single day to not being allowed to mention her name.

Good, Catholic girls never question their parents. That's what my mother cautioned, anyway. Pia was suddenly taboo, and I was a cruel daughter to mention her around my father. Or any of the Ingleciases, for that matter.

Maybe it's a testament to how damn sheltered I was—or how selfish—that I never really questioned it after the first few days. I pushed all thoughts of her, my best friend, to the back of my mind, and I did what we Pavalos do best.

I wore my brightest smile and conveyed to the world that I had no real care or thought in my head. I was happy, innocent Ada-Maria. The only skeletons in my closet were those literally written in the Holy Bible. I was an upstanding girl who never feared that her father raped and murdered her best friend and disposed of her family the way one would plastic utensils after a barbecue.

Because Pia is still alive, of course—she *has* to be.

Even though I know full well that my father is capable of the worst.

Somehow, Domino is connected to everything… Is blackmail his aim? Though, who is left to extort if he's killed Papa and has me captive?

I dwell on the thought, and I let the fear consume me. I sob openly and loudly, rocking myself against the mattress as tears fall hot and fast from my eyes to wet the sheets. I shiver, feeling every bruise and scrape throb at full force.

And with every cry, I'm reminded of the danger lurking beyond my thin white shroud. The collar is a constant presence, and I'm aware of the length of chain dangling from it always. Especially when it's suddenly yanked by an unseen hand.

Mid-sob, I'm silenced, forced to crawl toward the source of the pulling. From beyond my realm of blankets looms Domino Valenciaga. He stands at the foot of the bed, the chain in hand.

Panic sets in as I take in the room's interior. It looks different. No longer is the sunlight a bright golden hue, but a sultry orange glow paints the man before me bronze.

He's changed as well, switching the all-black ensemble for one of all white. Wearing a loose dress shirt and a pair of white slacks, he embodies my prior religious comparison to a fallen angel. This man is Lucifer himself, here to condemn me to hell.

On second thought, the devil comparison is too easy. Too simple. This man is something far, far worse. He is vengeance incarnate, as elusive as his supposed motives.

"You are ungrateful, you know that?" He doesn't sound angry. Not even when he turns his back to me to stare from the nearest window.

I didn't notice before, but this room has a breathtaking view of the terrace gardens from another angle. Here, the sunlight bathes the fields and fountains in varying hues of soothing ochre. It would be a vacation spot most would die to inhabit during the summer months. Overall, a beautiful prison.

"Selfish. Spoiled. None too bright. I knew this all, of course, even after all the time I've spent watching you from afar. Still, Ada-Maria, your complete lack of self-preservation astounds."

He's insulting me. The worst part is that I don't truly understand about what.

"Ines was to prepare you a nice bath, feed you a filling lunch, and allow you ample time to sleep. But you've wasted it."

He shrugs, turning to face me. "I was going to issue your punishment now and deny you those little comforts, but luckily for you, I am not as punitive as your father. Unfortunately, however, Ines is off for the evening, so she will be unable to assist you."

He pauses. I sense that he wants me to parse over his meaning. That I'll have to wash myself? Objectively, I haven't bathed without a maid in years, but I'm more than willing to make an exception now.

But no… That would be too simple. The reality of what he intends sinks in with the impact of a stabbing blade, and I bolt upright, feeling along the sheets for anything I can use as a barrier between us.

"Stay the hell away from me—"

"I have no qualms in filling in for her," Domino says, confirming my worst suspicion. Heedless of my refusal, he advances, lowering his gaze toward the mattress—I didn't even realize that I've gathered the length of my chain, holding it loosely in a fist. When he takes another step, I brandish it, but my hand shakes so badly it sways, rattling against itself.

"D-Don't touch me!"

"I suggest you save your fight for later, Ada-Maria," Domino warns, taking yet another step. "Trust me, I am more than eager to experience firsthand how much the daughter of Roy Pavalos values her life, and I'd prefer you not to exhaust yourself before then. But—"

He lunges. One of his hands snatches my forearm, shoving me facedown against the mattress. My heartbeat surges through my ears as I feel the metal snatched from my grasp. Without warning, my throat is wrenched from behind, raising my head from the bed as I gasp at the air.

"I think I'll bathe you, first," Domino murmurs as he maneuvers to stand before me, chain in hand. "I want you clean and dressed before dinner."

I'm flashed back to our last "meal." Who could he serve to me next? My mother?

"No!" I sink my nails into the sheets beneath me, digging my heels into the mattress.

I barely see his arm move before I'm lurching forward, hitting the floor on my knees, my ears ringing.

"Come," he says, manipulating the leash so that I lurch another inch across the floor. "I won't enjoy having your skin covered in bruises by the time I can enjoy you, Ada-Maria. At least, any that aren't inflicted by *me*."

I choke, horrified by the insinuation. Rape?

No, a childish part of me whispers. He'd have to be interested in me sexually for that. My cheeks flame when I replay all the times I would prance before him, hoping to grab his notice. When each attempt failed, I consoled myself with a logical explanation for his lack of interest in addition to taking his job too seriously—he is homosexual.

That pathetic attempt to soothe my own pride might be my sole salvation now. I cling to it, finding the strength to crawl after him as he marches toward the door.

The length of chain is about ten feet long, meaning he's already left the room by the time I stagger to my feet and follow.

Again, this strange dwelling takes on a newer identity depending on the time of day. At night, it's a fortress. By day, it's an ethereal wonderland, and during this twilight hour…

It's hell. Ignited by the glow cast by the setting sun, the walls gleam orange like flames. Everything takes on the reddish sheen, and with his white clothing, Domino resembles a creature composed of shadow and fire.

Without warning, he turns into a room just before we'd enter that circular foyer. I recognize it the second I cross the threshold after him—the bathroom Ines brought me to the other night.

Beside her, I'd been able to appreciate the beauty of it.

Domino's presence transforms the sleek design into a torture chamber. The gold fixtures are potential posts he can wrap my leash around, the walk-in shower a likely death trap. My mind spins, envisioning all of the many ways he can hurt me here. He wants to.

When he turns to me, I take a step back, shuddering at the look I see in his eyes.

But I forget that he has the leash in his grasp. He winds a few more inches around his wrist—a warning. The chain is a rigid line between us. Any more pressure, and he'll be choking me.

"A bath or a shower, Ada-Maria," he proposes. "Your choice."

"Shower," I blurt, preferring the barrier of a glass stall to having him stand over me in the tub.

He nods. To my shock, he releases the chain, letting it clang to the floor. Then he maneuvers around the room, gathering various supplies as he goes. From a golden rack of cream-colored towels, he takes one and fetches a bottle from beneath the countertop. Bounty in hand, he walks right past the shower stall to the tub. He runs the water, adjusting the drain to let it fill. Eyeing me from over his shoulder, he says, "A bath it is."

I grit my teeth, irritated to have fallen into his trap so easily.

"You can wait as I prepare it," he adds. "I'll undress you myself."

My feet twitch against the floor. He's at least four feet from the end of the chain. If I can drag it toward me in time, I might be able to make it through the door before he could catch me.

"Try to run," he says above the roar of the water. "Ines may be off this evening, but Pedro and Miguel are not. They've been forewarned to merely apprehend you, should you try to escape, no matter how violent your attempt might be. Have no fear, Ada-Maria—only *I* can inflict punishment upon that beautiful body."

Chills. Despair grips me, so overwhelming that I croak out a sob before I can stifle it. My heart aches. Every breath is a struggle, and I almost wish he'd grab that chain and choke me now. End this.

Instead, he sits on the rim of the tub, watching me as though my terror is an amusing show. I feel my knees buckle, threatening to pitch me to the floor while I'd beg him to let me go. I might do it too.

If a part of my brain wasn't stuck on that one word. I'm sure he meant it as a threat, but it sticks out regardless, diminishing the overall malice.

"I'm not beautiful…t-to you," I add hastily. My self-esteem never hinged on his notice—but if it did, my vanity would be nonexistent. "You never wanted me before."

"And you sound so damn proud of that, Ada-Maria. Like you've solved some million-dollar puzzle." He laughs while reaching back with one hand, dipping his fingers beneath the rising water. The amount of steam issuing from it already has me on edge, but he doesn't react as though it's scalding. Finished, he flicks his fingers at me one by one, spraying droplets of water onto the floor. "Trust a Pavalos to take pride in whether or not her attacker wants to fuck her. Because you've wanted me to for a long time, haven't you?"

I feel my cheeks catch fire. "N-No!"

"Liar." He levels his gaze over mine with a piercing intensity.

Too intense. I look away, and he laughs again.

"Don't think I haven't noticed all the times you've pranced past me in some skimpy little dress, hoping to have me drooling like the other men in your father's employ. It was always a game to you, wasn't it? Seeing how many you could get to fuck you. Want to fuck you. It's the only thing you had to look forward to in your sheltered, pathetic life. Has no one told you that beauty doesn't last forever, Ada-Maria?"

If they did, it was some bitchy blogger or a jealous cunt from primary school. My mother is the perfect, shining example that beauty can get you anywhere and last as long as you damn well want it to. Even if you had to claw at it with Botox injections, fillers, and liposuction. Beauty is a construct, she liked to say. One that she perfected how to wield to her benefit—at least while in public. Pretty makeup can hide everything, even sickness and decay.

"You're right. I never thought you were beautiful," Domino says.

I'm pathetic enough that the admission stings. Despite everything, I'm not immune to that one form of insult.

Rejection based on my appearance alone.

"Beauty is too delicate a word to describe what you are." He nods toward me and inclines his head. "I've changed my mind. Undress. Now."

My heart plummets through my body, hitting the floor. I can taste my own fear, as potent as blood. I don't know what I'll do. *Run,* I think, as my toes twitch again.

Then it creeps in—that sick, twisted voice whispering from the back of my mind. Undressing myself would be better than having him do it. He'd most likely rip the dress from my skin. This way, I can keep some modicum of decency.

Besides…

The only way men use moments like this to regain control is by using lust as a cudgel to induce fear. In this case, I don't have to worry about that.

I have the upper hand.

"The water's almost ready, Ada-Maria," he scolds. He snaps his fingers, and it's a second before I realize that he didn't intend to summon anyone. He only meant to spur me on.

My hands shake so badly I can barely hook them beneath the thin straps of the dress. I'm sloppy and rough, refusing to take my time or give him a show. Instead, I jerk the material over my head and throw it toward his feet.

I don't know why, but it feels more liberating than humiliating to stand here, knowing that I've defied at least one of his sick games. I don't cower.

Until he stands. The way he looks at me…

My fragile assessment of him shatters. That gleam in his eye isn't disinterest.

It's predatory.

"Stop." His command sinks into my body, rooting me in place before I even register moving. I'd been poised to take a step back, my foot still hovering above the floor.

"*Ay, Dios mío.* I always want to remember you like this," he rasps.

My pulse turns painful, every beat of my heart registering like the blow from a fist. *Thump. Thump.* Belatedly, I can recognize that there was no real admiration in his voice. Not like the way I'm used to men admiring me. With covetous need and naked desire.

Domino speaks of me in this moment like I'm a toy on display. The way men boast about a piece of property they own. Or, the way my father sounded on the night of his first political victory. Like this small triumph was the first step toward his ultimate goal—utter domination of the city, its people. Everything.

"Pink tweed skirt and matching jacket. A cream-colored tank top that displayed your navel despite the conservative dress code your father enforced in his office. Or at least, he wanted everyone else to believe he disapproved. I know for a fact that he told you what to wear. How to wear it. The mayor was meeting with him that day to discuss him potentially becoming a deputy during his next term. You were to catch his eye, and of course, you did."

I swallow hard, swaying as the memory catches me off guard. I can still see that day so clearly, just as he described it. Like a good, doting daughter, I intruded on an important business meeting to make some menial request—using the credit card for shopping was my reason that day, I think—but my real aim was whatever my father wanted to achieve by flaunting me before his opponent like prey. It was a game to him.

I think he got off on it, far more than I did anyway.

That day stands out to me for one reason alone. As I sauntered through my father's office—an upscale building

I'd visited enough times to know inside and out—a new figure stood guard outside the boardroom where Papa was holding his meeting.

One look at him, and I felt tense and hot in a way I'd never felt before. Like my clothing was too tight, and the room was too small. Sex was a chore I'd grown bored of attempting sober, but I couldn't help but wonder how this man would feel inside me. He was so tall I had to strain on tiptoe to get a better look at the hard planes of his face. His eyes were dark, shrouded by the brim of a straw cowboy hat he somehow wore without looking as stupid as he should have. The shadow cast by it enhanced his chiseled features, deepening the mystery of who he was and why he was there.

Struck dumb, I'd inspected the rest of him, forgetting my purpose for being there at all. Tight faded jeans that clung to his muscular thighs, supporting a distinct bulge straining around the zipper where his cock would be, and a loose denim shirt that did little to disguise the bulk lurking beneath…

Overall, he was the most handsome man I'd ever seen. When I remembered how to move, I approached him, swishing my hips the way my old friend once taught me, my head held high.

As his eyes roved in my direction, I fixed him with my most charming smile. The one I'd spent hours practicing before a mirror to nail down that fragile line between sexy and coy.

I wanted him to look at me the way the lecherous mayor in the next room soon would. I wanted those dark eyes to drink me in with a raw precision that warned he was undressing me with them. I wanted him to look at me as though he wanted to take me then and there. *Strange,* I remember remarking. I never craved that kind of reaction so badly before.

He was a different sort of man. Perhaps that was part of the allure. He wasn't a bold, rich bastard accustomed to taking who or whatever he wanted.

No, he was someone who would look at me like a prize he could never attain. Unless I wanted him to.

"Hello," I addressed him in my lightest, flirtiest tone of voice. I even offered him a manicured hand—fully expecting that, like most men I encountered, he would brush his lips across the back of it rather than shake it. *"My name is Ada—"*

"I didn't know it was you," the present-day Domino admits. He's closer, stroking his chin as the fact that I'm naked grows more real by the second. His heat acts like a battering ram, rivaling the warmth emanating from the tub. "Not Ada-Maria, the chubby little ugly duckling I remembered, fully grown into a swan. I'd heard the rumors that you were quite the little whore. Still, I never imagined..."

He stops, snagging a lock of my hair between two fingers. Slowly, he grinds the strands together and sighs.

"That little pink skirt... I wanted to fuck you in it then and there, Ada-Maria. I'd never seen an ass so fucking round. Tits the spitting image of what every woman these days goes under the knife to achieve. Lips so pink I could imagine you biting them as I fucked you deep. Never in my life had I wanted a woman like that. I could feel my cock straining like a motherfucker. My careful plan would have been ruined in a heartbeat—"

I'm holding my breath, feeling my lungs strain for air. The worst part is that I can hear the truth. In every word. Every grudging bit of inflection. He wanted me.

Two days ago, I would have been elated by hearing those very words.

"But then," he continues, "I heard your name. Ada, you said. As in Ada-Maria Pavalos. Nothing has ever killed my hard-on faster than hearing that. Consider it a gift, Ada. The sick, twisted, disgusting soul you are inside is revolting enough to override a body designed by the Gods and a face so beautiful it's sin."

Shakily, I suck in air, hating just how deeply the insult wounds. I hear the words of my therapist, playing in a mocking loop. *You have low self-esteem, Ada. You seem to equate your sexuality and beauty directly to your self-worth. I'm sure that if you looked deep within yourself, you would find plenty of attributes worthy of being proud of. You are more than a pretty face...*

The bitch was wrong, of course. I knew that without having to hear Domino state it so bluntly. I'm empty inside. A shell over which my father would paint whatever he wanted me to be in that moment. Doting daughter. Dutiful doll.

A prize he could use to sway men to his side. Like the Mayor he met with that day. I spent that very night on my knees, choking down his cum with the same simpering smile on my face I'd attempted to charm Domino with. I think I would have fucked him even if Papa didn't tell me to; so fragile was my pride in the moments after I'd entered that boardroom.

"Hello," I told the man waiting by the door. *"I'm Ada."*

His dark eyes flickered, but not with lust or an ounce of interest. To my utter embarrassment, he looked away. Then he opened the door for me.

"Good morning, Ada-Maria."

Just that. Good morning in a flat, emotionless baritone. No innuendo. No flustered response. As shameful as it feels to admit in this present moment, I'd never felt uglier then. Not even during all those years as the "fat ugly duckling," so awkward my father had no use for me.

Wait…

"How did you know?" Returning to the present is like surfacing from minutes spent underwater. I'm breathless, panting after every word. "My weight… How?"

No one knew that. It was a time in my life when my father had no use for me. Overweight with braces, cystic acne, and poor grades, it was more beneficial to him to have me shipped off from boarding school to boarding school.

I had no one in those days. Just Pia and one other friend.

The three amigas.

"How did you know?" I ask, facing Domino. My father could have told him, but I doubt that. I personally went through our family photos and ripped up any that featured me in that state. I only kept one in a safe place no one else could find.

"Know what?" His tone shifts again. Did I catch him off guard? If so, his face stubbornly gives nothing away. "That you were a chubby, awkward teenager? It's not exactly an unusual origin story for a woman as superficial as you. Anyone could take one look at you and know that."

But they'd have to strip me to do so.

I remember crying into my pillow every night, praying that I could go through a growth spurt capable of adding inches to my height while subtracting double from my waist. Pia was so pretty in comparison to me. Standing beside her, was like being reduced to a piece of scenery. All eyes went to her. Men, women, adults, and children alike. Beautiful Pia, with her enchanting hazel eyes, slender frame, and dark hair, could light up a room with just a smile.

The same smile I stole from her years after her disappearance. I spent hours in the mirror trying to get it just right. But I never could.

For ten years, I've held a secret I wasn't brave enough to confess even to my therapist. That on my fifteenth birthday, I stood next to Pia, and I made a wish as I blew out my candles. Just one. No longer did I dream for another pony, or new clothes, or Daddy's affection.

I just wanted to be like *her*. As beautiful as her. As tall and as skinny.

As desirable.

A week later, she went missing, and six months after that, I shot up five inches and lost forty pounds almost overnight.

But no one tells you that Cinderella was the only bitch in the world to undergo a transformation without scars to show for it. Rapid weight loss leaves tiny little silvery stretch marks that speckle the skin like veins. No matter how much you scrub, buff, or pay for laser removal treatments, they never go away.

The men who fuck you years later might trace them with their fingers, sensing the slight flaws in your seemingly perfect skin. *Were you hurt?* One of them asked me once.

He didn't really care as to the answer.

My cunt worked, at least.

"Did you hear me?"

I shiver as thick, calloused fingers slip beneath my chin, gripping it tight until I face the man before me, my eyes streaming.

"I asked if you like it hot or cold."

I blink, confused. "W-What?"

"The water." He snatches my collar, sliding his finger beneath the thin leather. With a beckoning motion, he yanks me forward so suddenly I nearly trip into him.

At the last moment, he pivots, shoving me aside.

Whoosh! Water hits my skin, so hot, every ounce of air leaves my chest. A hard surface slams against my knee as I scramble to brace my hands against something firm, but curved, beneath me. The bottom of the tub? My head, however, is still above water, my mouth open. I'm trying to scream, but I can't even make a sound.

"Too hot?" Domino questions as he shuts the faucet off. "Don't," he warns when I grip the rim, ready to bolt from the basin. "I suggest you endure it, Ada-Maria. Think of it as practice for what else I have in store for you."

"You're sick." My reply is a wail, barely audible beneath the pain.

Everything hurts. My skin is raw, blistering wherever it contacts the water. I'm burning alive. More tears fall, and I'm helpless to stop them.

"You're a monster—"

"I'd advise you to save the insults," Domino suggests. He sits on the rim of the tub and plunges his hand beneath the water. Leisurely he feels down to the bottom, dipping between my legs.

I jump, bracing myself to feel his touch, but he evades my skin completely, retrieving something with a sigh. The chain. Deliberately, he loops it around and around his wrist, seemingly unbothered by the scalding heat.

"I have a lot more planned for you, Ada-Maria," he says once the majority of the chain is secured, leaving me just enough to breathe freely. "This is merely an act of mercy. Later, you'll thank me for seeing that you are fed and bathed. I will bet my life on that. This will be the last luxury your beautiful skin will feel for a long while. Now…" He bends, fiddling with something that must be on the floor by his feet. When he sits upright, he's holding a bottle of different colored liquid in either hand.

"Honey or Lavender?"

Body wash, I presume. Each one looks to be a golden liquid at the base, with one containing purple flowers, and the other simmering bits of pearlescent beads.

Eyeing them, I shiver so violently water sloshes over the rim. He couldn't know. Could he?

But those choices are so specific. So deliberately plotted. God, these memories hurt more than they should. It's been so damn long. Why can I still hear her so clearly, her laughter infectious?

Purple is the color of royalty, Adie. So is gold. They'll be our colors, the three queens…

"Pia," I croak, swiping at my cheek to banish whatever tears I can. "You knew Pia."

He looks away and makes a show of lifting each bottle for closer observation.

But I don't miss the satisfied tilt to his mouth. This test I passed with flying colors.

"Pia Inglecias," he murmurs. "I've heard the story. Who hasn't? What a damn shame for that poor girl and her family."

Her family.

"She only had her mother," I say. But the second the words leave my mouth, I realize I'm wrong. "And a brother, but he —" I break off, feeling my throat go dry at the possibility. Could he somehow be a living Inglecias? It could explain his grudge. Even as I think it, I recall a detail that renders that explanation impossible. "He was sick. With a terminal heart condition. It couldn't be cured."

Whenever Pia spoke of him, it was briefly, only to mention how precarious his health was. *My brother was the fastest runner in the neighborhood before he got sick. Could have gone to play ball in the big leagues, I bet. That's why I'm here,* she added, referring to our boarding school. It was an open secret that she was there on a scholarship as part of the school's community outreach toward promising students from poor families. *Mama is too busy with Nav to worry about me, too. I'm not jealous, though. He needs the help.*

As far as I knew, his life expectancy was months by the time we both turned fifteen. Even if he did manage to live, I doubt a boy who survived a congenital heart defect, so severe he could no longer run, would grow into a man sculpted from solid muscle.

He's been listening to me speak all this time, but I can't gauge a single hint of emotion.

"A brother," he says. "Funny. From what I remember, Pia Inglecias was an only child."

I shake my head. "No, I remember—"

"Lift your arms." When I don't comply fast enough, he snaps his fingers. "Now, Ada-Maria. As much as another man would enjoy the sight of your naked body, I find that the allure has worn off—" he inspects me with a ruthless sweep of his gaze, his eyes narrowing. "It's not quite as impressive as I imagined."

Because he *did* imagine me once. Five years ago, before he knew who I was, when I sauntered up to him wearing a pink ensemble with a cream top. He wanted me then.

But not now. No man can fake this level of disinterest. Like the vain creature I am, I cling to the same excuse I've used all these years to explain it. *He's gay.* There is nothing wrong with that.

It just means, in the grand scheme of his nefarious plans, I have nothing to fear when it comes to the realm of sexual violence. …Right?

Slowly, I lift my arms without taking my eyes off his face.

He bends, grabbing something else from the materials at his feet—a cream-colored cloth. He makes a show of wetting it with the bathwater, barely grazing my knee with the fabric. Then he comes at me directly.

I stiffen, hating the way my body reacts to him. Part of it is instinctive. The rest is pure vanity. It's repulsive how his appearance can still have an effect on me.

He's handsome beneath the evil, and my brain struggles to separate the two. Why would it? I've spent my entire life in the shadow of a man who excelled at blending beauty with violence.

And therein lies the key to resisting him and dampening any attraction I may feel. Those in my father's orbit always joked that Domino was his shadow, damn near inseparable from his master. They were wrong, of course.

Domino is no better than my father, bred from the same stock all powerful, egotistical men are born from.

"What are you thinking behind those eyes, Ada-Maria?" His tone is so deceptively casual that a part of me is lulled by it. I respond to him without thinking.

"That you seem to hate my father, but you're just like him—"

I break off the second I see his arm move. My body braces for another slap, but when his finger does make contact with my face, it's gently, stroking along the corner of my mouth.

"You will never compare me to him again, do you understand?" His eyes hunt mine ruthlessly, reminding me of a stern father scolding a naughty child. "Do you?"

I'm terrified enough to nod—but as I do, my lips part. Curiosity is as addicting as any other vice when it comes to him.

"Why?" My eyes water, and blinking frees more tears despite how hard I try to keep them at bay. It's horrifying to think of all the ways he's been invited into the very heart of my family, becoming a regular fixture at my mother's perfunctory Sunday dinners. "You worked for him for five years," I add. "Why now?"

I think of all the times I snuck glances at him, imagining how that body would feel against mine. Was I so naïve as to not sense his true feelings? Was I just blind to the hate lurking beneath that stern façade?

Or just stupid enough to be easily fooled.

"Why?" He taps his thumb against my bottom lip, applying a bit more pressure with each pass. I hiss as he nears the throbbing mark from his slap. "You're right. For five years, I worked for the bastard. I hid his messes. Cleaned up his dirty work—"

"You killed for him." It's an accusation I've never made out loud, but one I know full well is the damn truth.

He doesn't try to deny it. "I did. I arranged hits on the political enemies he wanted out of the way. I sent covert threats to their families. I handled his contacts with the men who ran his drug mules in and out of the city. I covered up every illicit affair while your Mama's back was turned—"

I wrench away from him, eyeing the floor. Harshly, he snatches my chin, forcing me to face him.

"He had a type," he tells me, his voice gruffer. Guttural. "Some could say it was creepily specific. He liked them young with supple tanned skin, and big round eyes—bonus points if they were light blue, or even gray. He liked big tits, a tiny waist, and long, straight hair, preferably blond—"

"You're disgusting!"

He chuckles and dips the hand holding the cloth into the water just beyond my quivering belly.

"I'm not the man who liked fucking women who resemble his daughter, Ada-Maria."

Is he lying? Bile spills up my throat and I can't process the thought further. I squeeze my eyes shut instead, struggling to keep my breathing steady. I can't give in to the panic now. It's what he wants. He's trying to rattle me.

It's working.

"Don't tell me you didn't sense that his devotion to his only daughter verged on the unhealthy," Domino taunts.

When I open my eyes, he's smirking. He's gotten inside my head, and he knows it. Even if my father were screwing other women on the side, that has nothing to do with me. Nothing.

"I guess that means he molded you into the perfect woman according to him. Beauty. Obedient. No brains to speak of. The only downside was that he couldn't touch you, so he had to make do somehow." Withdrawing his hand from my chin, he uses both to wring the water from the cloth. Then he brings it to my chest as if daring me to react.

I do, flinching as the fabric makes contact. It's painful to subject myself to his touch. He swipes across the top of my breasts and dips the cloth into the water again.

"I'll spare you what the rumors have claimed about you and your dearest Don Roy. I hope, in that case, it was all merely talk—"

"You don't know anything!" My voice is a whisper, strained by how badly I'm shaking. Every secret I've kept at bay cloys on the tip of my tongue like a bad taste.

My father never abused me. Sexually.

But sex was always a game to me. A trivial act, neither overly fun or too boring to attempt every now and again. I never felt the rapture other women bragged about. I was damn good at faking it like I did, though. Sex never terrified me the way it did good, seemingly wholesome girls like Pia who openly fantasized about the man they would bestow their virginity upon.

I want a love like in the movies, she told me once. *Real tragic shit. I want to orgasm rainbows and live happily ever after…*

Deep down, I think I've always believed that there are other forms of violation far more degrading than sex. A body can heal.

The mind can't. I was never one to play the "my trauma was worse" card like some of the spoiled bitches from my boarding school, who equated credit card limits with child abuse, liked to. Still, I tend to believe that I'm smart enough to recognize that there are some lines a normal parent shouldn't cross. "Favors," they should never ask of their children.

Secrets they should never demand be kept.

"Your father never touched you," Domino declares, but when I look up…

He's scanning my face intently, and I get that niggling feeling again. He's telling me what he believes he knows. What he wants to hear. Anything otherwise goes against the narrative he's built.

"How did you kill him?" I don't think I really want to know the answer. Somehow, it feels important just to say it. To watch his expression shift as he mulls over his reply.

I think I'm hoping to catch him up. To prove that it's a lie. Papa is alive and well, and the nightmare that has ruled my life wouldn't end so easily.

Domino cocks his head. "It was slow," he tells me, his voice surprisingly expressive. He doesn't sound like someone recounting a traumatic event. He sounds like a man re-living a sweet, beautiful moment he wants to savor reminiscing. "Very slow, Ada-Maria. Over hours. He suffered, if that's what you really wanted to know. He suffered greatly."

I close my eyes again, inhaling raggedly. A wave of emotions crashes over me, but the worst part? I can't decide which one to feel; they all resonate with the same intensity. Horror. Grief. Pain. Relief…

"Turn around so I can finish," Domino demands, cutting my mourning short.

I comply in silence, too stunned to question.

"Wait—"

He grabs my arm, dragging me toward him, and I scream, reflexively trying to escape his grasp.

"No."

Something in his voice freezes me solid. I go still as he yanks me to my knees with my back to him.

The water drips from my body, playing an eerie melody as I brace myself for his assault. Will he hurt me now? I almost can't stifle another scream as cool air tickles my ass, warning of an impending touch.

Instead, he prods my lower back, and my confusion battles with the terror. Then I realize exactly what he's inspecting.

Oh, that.

"You were whipped," he says, his voice rough as he drags the pad of his finger over a long-healed scar. It's one of many. "Multiple times… By who?"

CHAPTER SEVEN

You were whipped...

The anger in his voice seems alarmingly out of place. My breath catches as I weigh the possibility that my scars somehow offended him. They're so small, that I was assured surgery wouldn't be needed to erase them. In fact, few have ever pointed them out, at least not to me.

And not like this.

"I... I thought you knew everything there was to know about me?" I rasp. Especially since he spent more time with my father than anyone. He would know exactly what a man like Roy Pavalos is capable of.

"Apparently not," he replies. Hot like a poker, his finger traces one of the linear scars, triggering a memory I try to ignore.

Pain, sharp and stinging. The chilling hiss of leather snapping at the air. My own screams...

"Were you? Whipped?"

I flinch at the question, phrased so differently than the first time. Like he wants me to confirm it. This hint of violence clashes with the fictional version of Ada Pavalos he's formed in his head. I'm so sure of what he thinks of me—a dumb slut who never had to work a day in her life. No way could the scars on her back be anything more than a harmless accident.

"I fell into a cactus on a trip to the desert," I blurt tonelessly, shrugging his fingers aside.

It's funny how little I've said that lie in comparison to how many days I spent poring over every detail to make it believable. How much information to give. How much to withhold. How to make my tone the right mix of bored and embarrassed to sell it.

I've gotten so good that I've fooled myself.

I even fool him.

He withdraws, bored by the marks. No part of me holds his interest, I see when I sneak a glance at him from over my shoulder. Even naked, I might as well be a part of the wall.

Shame bites deep despite every ounce of logic in my brain warning me that this is a good thing. I don't *want* to appeal to him. Being seen as unattractive by a monster should be a blessing. It shouldn't sting.

"Get up." He's on his feet again, crossing over to the counter. From a drawer, he withdraws a silver brush similar to the one Ines used on me earlier. I shudder at the thought of how he might go about such a task.

When I climb from the tub, I spot the towel he procured, resting on the floor, just beyond my reach. I take a step toward it.

"No." Domino snaps his fingers. "Not yet. Come."

The floor is slick enough to make every step a struggle. I slide the second I try to move, flailing my arms to stay upright.

I don't know if he takes pity on me, or if it's a willingness to adhere to his "schedule" that makes him approach me himself, brush in hand.

"Look forward."

I cringe as he raises the brush, expecting the worst. As the first stroke runs through my hair, some of the tension in my muscles loosens. Some. He's as briskly efficient as Ines, and when he's smoothed every last strand, he grabs the towel himself.

I reach for it, hoping he'll let me dry myself. Ignoring my outstretched hand, he steps behind me, dragging the towel over my back. Then across my ass and down my thighs.

I think the fact that I'm waiting for the cruelty is why the softness of his touch catches me off guard. He's methodic, working just enough pressure into my skin as he goes to soothe the muscles underneath. As the cooler night air tickles my body in contrast to the heat of the water, his ministrations, paired with the quality of the towel's material, have me relaxing before I can help it.

Everyone knows how violent physical pain can be. How aching limbs can throb and sting. Few people ever recognize that the worst part can come afterward. When the very person responsible for inflicting those aches and pains is the same one who takes it upon themselves to soothe them. It does something to a person's mind, to have the source of brutality provide comfort.

My body is already conditioned to the dichotomy. That's why I arch into his next pass that travels from my lower back down to my thigh, raising goosebumps. I don't know exactly when it happens…

When I start to twist along with his movements as he dries off my legs. I have no control over how my nerves prickle with the awareness of him. How my breathing hitches the lower he goes.

My eyes are closing without permission from my brain. For a second, it's almost too easy to teleport myself somewhere else. But where? Clara would never touch me like this— swiftly but with a subtle, teasing intimacy that feels too hostile to match any prior lover of mine, either. No.

Those men worshiped me. Used me. Groped.

Domino…

He toys with me. Plays me the way my father would his old guitar when he felt the need to show off during a dinner party. Like any good entertainer, he knew how to create hype with every stroke of the strings. How to build anticipation by drawing out every second he spent tuning the instrument, well before he began performing in earnest.

I hate myself for how easily Domino can turn my own body against me. Conspiratorially, his heat eats through the towel, coaxing my limbs into submission. I'm suddenly aware of every breath expanding my lungs, filling my chest. I can feel each nipple tighten in the next breeze to blow in from the open windows. I can smell him. Taste his scent mingling with the aroma of the body wash he used on me —*lavender.*

It's like I'm drugged on the stench of it all. I forget the source responsible for the creeping pressure inching up my inner thigh. I forget that I should shy away from it.

I spread my thighs instead…

"Jesus Christ, Ada-Maria." The disgust in his voice hits me like a slap.

I wrench my eyes open as shame floods my cheeks.

"I knew you were a whore, but damn." He pushes past me, dropping the towel on the floor. Angry, fierce strides carrying him into the hall before the full weight of my embarrassment has a chance to sink in.

What the hell is wrong with me? I've become accustomed to training my body to react separately from my brain. To endure the touch of greedy, grasping old men, or drooling sycophants of my father. I've perfected how to smother every ounce of discomfort. How to turn pain into pleasure. I know how to fake and fake and *fake*.

But my heartbeat hammers out a mocking beat as if to taunt me with the truth.

Thump. You weren't faking. Thump.

"I said come."

The command lashes at the air, and a sense of foreboding erases all traces of his touch. I don't think I've ever heard that note in his voice before. That cold, detached hiss.

Run, Ada.

I stoop for the towel and drape it over my torso as I creep to the doorway and flick my eyes in the direction opposite the way he went. I should run now. Try to escape. A part of me knows deep down that to try at all would be a waste. Still, I can't shake the sense that I should, if only to prove to him that I can.

And to myself.

"Run," he calls to me as if reading my mind. I stiffen, puzzled by the prospect of him giving me permission to escape. "And you will sorely regret it. My patience is running thin Ada-Maria. *Come!*"

Left with no choice, I shuffle toward the voice, swallowing hard the closer I come. I finally find him in that white room, only now—considering the sun has fully set and darkness officially fallen—it's silvery in appearance, illuminated by a crystalline chandelier above.

It's been transformed in my absence—a pointed reminder that we aren't alone here. There are other servants in addition to Ines. During my bath, they stripped the bed and replaced the sheets with an identical set devoid of blood. A long, rectangular gift box, wrapped in white and topped with a matching bow, rests near the foot of the mattress. A present?

The floor has been polished to shine and in the center of the space now rests the same white table he offered me "tea" on earlier. Now, it's laden with a platter of white fish, a bowl of salad, and a basket of steaming rolls.

Rather than smirk at me from a seated position, Domino stands with his back to me, his gaze on the window.

"Eat," he snaps, and my unease grows. He's angry, but as I replay the incident from the bathroom in my mind, I don't think he should be. If anything, he should be gloating. I played into his narrative of a dumb, stupid whore.

The nerves contribute to how my stomach twists at the smell of the food. I can taste the freshness of the fish just from its aroma—but I don't dare trust it. Or him.

I quash the gnawing hunger pains, reclaiming my flimsy grasp on control. Meeting his gaze, I lie without an ounce of guilt, "I'm not hungry."

"I suggest you draw out your reprieve as long as you possibly can, Ada-Maria," he warns in a tone that stops my blood cold. "Now sit down and eat!"

I stagger to a chair and collapse onto it, reaching for a fork, only to fumble and send it—and the rest of the silverware by it—clattering to the floor.

My eyes cut to him, my lungs paralyzed. Seconds tick by, but he doesn't react.

Because he's dwelling on something, I suspect. Somehow, I offended him, more than just by responding to his touch. But how?

I bite my lip at the sensation washing through me. It's painfully familiar. Ironic, in a sense. Papa is supposedly dead, but this man can make me feel the same way only he could.

On pins and needles, dancing on eggshells around a mood as volatile as a summer storm.

"I don't hear you eating."

I grab the fork, as well as the knife and spoon. Hastily, I assemble a plate, noisily scraping each platter as I go to prove that I'm obeying.

Once my plate is full, however, I can no longer play pretend. Impulsively, I resort to my tried-and-true method for making it through one of my family's mandated dinners.

I stab at a piece of lettuce and drag it across the porcelain plate to a distant corner. Then I cut the fish into squares.

Quarters. Then those chunks into smaller slivers. Flakes. Mush. I spread it across my plate in random sections to make it look like I've picked through it. The bread I rip into three pieces and try to crumble them as small as possible.

It's a convincing effort when all is said and done—or at least it *would* be.

If I didn't look up a heartbeat later to find him watching me, his arms crossed, gaze unreadable. Gradually, his expression morphs from callous to interested. Then enraged.

He moves too quickly to muster a defense. All I can do is cringe into my seat as he snatches my plate from the table and hurls it against the wall. *Wham!* The porcelain shatters as the food speckles the floor in a colorful display.

"I've shown you mercy, Ada-Maria," he snarls that word as though it's the most coveted gift in all the world. Mercy from him. "I gave you time to heal from your journey here. I offer you nourishment. I bathe you. Give you clothing. I ask you nicely for what it is I'm after. And this is how you repay me?"

He's shouting, his voice booming. Brutally, he snatches the towel from me. A hard shove pushes me from the chair to the ground. I cry out, wincing as my sore thigh aches with the impact. Instinct takes priority, urging me to my knees. *Cower.* The way I have so many times before, I scurry from the threat, staring only at the floor before me.

Move, Ada. Move!

"You play fucking mind games," Domino snarls. "No more. I've decided that it's time for your punishment."

"D-Don't!" I cover my head as his steps resonate through the floor, but they blow past me. Through trembling fingers, I watch him approach the bed instead.

He grabs the "present," ripping off the lid. The box, he throws aside, revealing what it contained, brandished in his fist.

"N-No…" I've never heard my voice sound like this. This weak. Then again, I have—just in those memories I've pushed to the back of my mind, never to revisit. "Don't!"

I'm on my feet, racing toward the door with a single-minded focus.

I don't even see him coming.

Wham! I hit the floor on my side, unsure of what struck me. Or where. The air wheezes from my lungs as specks of light dot my vision. A shadow moves from the corner of my eye. His hand.

He grabs my hair, yanking me onto my stomach.

"I said, on your knees."

I rush to comply, toppling over twice in my attempt. When I look up, he's standing over me, that thing trailing from his hand to graze the floor.

It's a whip. Brand-new, made of braided black leather that fans into a tail of three separate points. They're naked—not tipped with metal, thank God—but I know that the pain is only *slightly* less. The wounds won't scar the same way. But God, will it hurt.

"Please, don't—"

"You were twenty-two minutes late the first night," he growls. With a flick of his wrist, he extends the whip. "You ignored Ines' request. For that, I will double your tally. And after the stunt you just pulled…"

His eyes glow, and I know there's no point in running.

I go numb, crying silent tears as he moves to stand behind me. His shadow paints the floor, illustrating exactly what he's doing—not that I need the visual.

Crack! He tests the whip against the air with a sound that draws a whimper from my chest.

"Please don't—"

"You try to run, and I'll add fifty more lashes for every attempt. You brought this upon yourself."

Fire. It's like being severed in two, this kind of pain. My brain disconnects from my body, and I'm just a bystander watching a pathetic, sniveling creature at the mercy of someone else.

One.

"Your father coddled you like a fucking child your entire life, and you obeyed him, didn't you? His perfect little girl?"

Two.

I groan as three individual lines catch the flesh clinging to my spine. It hurts. So badly…

I was wrong before. He is nothing like my father.

Roy drew out my punishments sadistically with an enviable sense of control. He rarely gave in to rage from the outset. It was a game with him. How long could he maintain restraint? Always right until I'd least expect it.

"You helped him!"

Three.

Seven.

Eleven.

"You helped him kill her, didn't you? Didn't you?"

On the one hand, I know that Domino's voice is in my ear, booming and gruff with rage. At the same time, another voice overlays him.

"You've made me do this, you understand? You aren't held to the same standard as those other little bastards. You are a Pavalos!"

"P-Please."

Another blow drowns out the plea.

Fifteen…

Or is it seventeen?

"Not a day goes by when I don't fucking regret letting your mother carry you to term. You are a disappointment, Ada. A fucking disgrace! Say that you deserve this. Say it!"

"I'm sorry." I go prone, pressing my forehead to the floor. I'm sobbing openly, snot mingling with the tears. It's what he wants, so I cry and rock back and forth with the pain. I put on a show; I give in to the fear. "I'm sorry. I'm sorry! I deserve it; I'm sorry. Please, Papa—"

"Jesus Christ."

I blink, confused. That voice isn't like Roy's. Never before would he relent this early. No. I'd need to repent for longer, and far more earnestly than that. I'd need to prove without a doubt that I deserved his forgiveness.

No matter how much blood he drew.

Thud!

I flinch, gritting my teeth against the next searing pain.

But it doesn't come. The only sound to follow is the slap of footsteps retreating from the room, into the hall.

When I finally contort myself to peek around my arm, I realize he's gone. Domino—because my father was never here. Nearby, the whip rests discarded on the floor, and I crawl in my rush to scurry as far from it as I can. My hip strikes the wall, and I finally take stock of the agony radiating up and down my back.

He lacked the cruel precision of Papa. He was ruthless. Reckless. My back feels sticky, my flesh so raw that it hurts to even attempt to stand or sit upright.

So, I curl into a ball and breathe through the agony.

He'll return soon enough.

He never finished counting.

CHAPTER EIGHT

"Good morning, Miss."

I peel my eyes open, alarmed when all I see is white. This iteration is a beautiful color, reflecting snippets of gold like rays of the sun. I must be dead. Only heaven could be this peaceful and this blindingly clean.

But then I feel the pain. It's dulled—which confuses me even more. Fiery, stinging lines throb all across my back, but it's as if an invisible hand is holding the worst at bay, allowing just a fraction of the discomfort to bother me. I recognize this dreamy, dazed mental state, where my brain feels like mush, and everything sparkles.

He drugged me again.

He drugged me *good*.

As a result, any fear I might feel is reduced to three tiny butterflies fluttering around in my belly, but I can still feel it, nonetheless; a prickling bit of instinct warning that I should be worried. I should question what he drugged me with and why. I should run.

"Mr. Domino requested that I treat your back again, Miss. Apologies."

Again?

I test my muscles experimentally and groan. My back is ablaze, but the rest of me isn't too far off. I hurt all over. The kind of pulsing discomfort I'd need an entire bottle of wine to dull completely.

The more I move, however, the more of my surroundings I'm able to take in. Heaven turns out to be the same white room I've been relegated to since arriving here. Beyond the bed, the picturesque illusion shatters.

My entire body goes cold the second I spot the white table a few feet away. It's in the same position as last night, though devoid of the food and only one chair remains. Someone took pains to clear the broken plate from the floor at least, though the wall still holds the multi-colored traces of where my meal shattered against it.

Domino isn't anywhere in sight—a fact that rips a sigh of relief from me.

But Ines stands on the opposite side of the bed, her hands folded before her. Within her reach is a white case placed on the edge of the mattress. Medical supplies?

"Miss?" She prompts. Apparently, she needs my permission this time.

I nod, jerking around to lie on my stomach again, facing the foot of the bed.

She moves gently, prodding my back to assess the damage. Only now do I realize that I'm still naked.

"Mr. Domino is away today," Ines explains while smoothing a cool liquid across my back. When it makes contact with the sorer areas, I flinch, but it's soothing, killing what little pain remains damn near instantly. Only when she's covered half of the affected area, do I fully register what she said.

And *how* she said it, phrased carefully as if inviting me to question.

"Where?" The second I speak, I'm reminded of the collar around my throat—and the chain neatly coiled a few inches from my head. The sight of it sends my heart plummeting, risking the peaceful mind state the drug is trying to set. No high could make this situation tenable.

"He will be gone until the evening," Ines adds. "Until then, he said that you are allowed to explore from the limits of the house, the terrace gardens, and the courtyard. You are to not go beyond the inner garden or the courtyard. Understood?"

I ignore her direct question the way she did mine. "Where are we? Why am I here?"

"Mr. Domino also requested that you enjoy lunch without him. He will require your presence at dinner. If you need anything, I am to assist you."

Her words all contain a monotone, practiced quality. I can't shake the sense that this is a speech she's rehearsed to death. Or one she's given many times before.

I twist my back as much as I dare and lift my head to face her. If she notices my staring, she goes out of her way to pretend not to. With careful, clinical precision, she dips what looks like a cotton swab into the mouth of a bottle of clear liquid, then applies that liquid to the remaining marks.

I hiss through my teeth at the sight of them—at least twenty lashes centered along my spine. Despite their angry, red appearance, I can tell that they aren't as deep as they look—only a few managed to rip through the deepest layers of skin, enough to bleed.

Ines doesn't bat an eyelash at the sight of them, cleaning each one with the same abject boredom I'd assume she scrubs the floor with.

"Your lunch will be ready in an hour," she says after swabbing the last open wound. "Until then, I recommend that you enjoy some sun. Though…" Her voice shifts, and something in me perks up to listen. For the first time, she meets my gaze directly, and all I see in her eyes is a desperate warning. "I would suggest you adhere to Mr. Domino's limits."

I swallow hard, blinking rapidly. I've already experienced the consequences of testing his "limits" once.

"Thank you," I croak.

Nodding, Ines returns the bottle of liquid to her white case. Then she gathers up the used cotton rounds in a plastic bag. "I will find you when lunch is ready to be served—"

"Wait!" I roll over to face her, scrambling to cover myself with most of the sheet. "Why am I here? What is he going to do with me? Help me…"

"Enjoy your day, Miss," Ines says, her head bowed respectfully. "I will find you when lunch is ready to be served."

Dejected, I watch her leave, feeling a sob build in my chest. When the tears fall, I marvel at their searing warmth. This is the most I've cried in…

Well, Pavalos aren't allowed to cry. Not in my father's presence, at least. We suffer in silence and endure any pain with bright smiles on our faces. *It's how we've survived for so long,* he used to say. No one could ever tell when we were wounded.

These days, wounds can heal into ugly marks easily lasered away or fixed with a simple surgery. Through it all, you just keep smiling.

"Oh, Mr. Domino requested one last thing." Ines scuttles back into the room, this time without her case.

I watch her cross over to the floor-length mirror she brushed my hair in front of the other day. She feels along the edge of it, revealing that the entire surface is really a door. It opens inward, into another room that she hurries inside.

Confused, I stand and follow her, limping with every step, though I still don't feel any real pain.

Perhaps, I'm far too distracted to. The doorway opens into a decent-sized walk-in closet.

And my throat goes dry.

He's had to have had many, many women here before—all of them the same stature as I am. There are so many dresses. Numerous shoes. The further I tiptoe into the closet, and the more I inspect each garment I pass, the more confused —and terrified—I become.

They're expensive. I note several distinct seasons from notable designers all within the past four years. Each one is the exact opposite of what my father would allow me to wear. Too edgy. Too dark, with most of the clothing falling into the range of black, cream, and white…

And one lone garment in red.

"He wants you to wear this one," Ines explains, holding up the delicate silk dress displayed on a golden hanger.

"What if I don't want to wear it?" I croak. Perhaps as an experiment to see how Ines will react.

All she does is meet my gaze and offer the dress to me. "Mr. Domino insists that you wear this one."

She must see the defeat in my face, because she finally advances and helps me pull the dress on. Gently, she smooths it over my hips, and I follow her from the closet to stare into the mirror.

It's objectively beautiful, but wearing it, the scarlet hue feels more like a death sentence. An ominous forewarning of what's to come. Domino Valenciaga plans on killing me. Perhaps in this very dress.

But intimidation wasn't his only reason for choosing it.

Ines motions for me to turn, and in the mirror, I glimpse the ensemble's unique features that make wearing it more prudent than threatening—it's backless. The material droops dramatically, falling down my hips and following the curve of my ass so that every mark from the whip is on display.

Like he planned each one as he went for the best effect. In his world, victims don't hide their scars. They wear them like some sick accessory for all to see.

"Lunch will be ready in an hour," Ines says, heading for the hallway again. "You can go."

I sense that the words convey permission and a subtle restraint in the same breath. Go, explore to my heart's content—but never forget that Mr. Domino wishes me to.

I eye the bed again, tempted to crawl beneath the covers and hide. Ignore his wishes and his plans. Let him come whip me.

Fear alone isn't what finally drives me from the room in the same direction Ines disappeared in. It's smart to take any opportunity I can to explore and plot an escape. I can't stay here.

I can't.

I've barely gone five feet from my room, however, before I realize that leaving this place might be easier said than done.

I'm already lost.

This section of the hall is long and winding with a row of windows overlooking the terrace but few doors that lead to spacious rooms and little else. I have to retrace my steps back to the bedroom and then retread the same ground Domino led me through last night to find my way back to that circular room.

So far, I know that one set of arches leads to the terrace. The other, to my room and the bathroom. A third takes me down a wide white hallway bathed in sunlight, and I stumble past the dining room. At the end of the corridor is a set of double doors, but they're locked. The entrance?

I don't think so.

I return to the archway and approach the remaining arch I haven't tested yet. It's a short entryway leading to a massive, ornately carved set of wooden double doors, curved at the top and nearly as tall as the ceiling. I reach for one of its two golden handles and tug half-heartedly, fully expecting it to be locked.

But it isn't.

It opens easily, revealing a different exit to the outdoors apart from the terrace. Tanned paved stones form a path around a bubbling fountain and through neatly trimmed hedges and tended beds of orange and red flowers in full bloom. It's as beautiful as the rest of the estate, but my heart lurches excitedly as I step beyond the house and realize that the path goes on until it abruptly meets a dirt road. A driveway?

My hands shake as I head in that direction on bare feet. There's no one in sight. No cars. No guards. Could escape truly be so easy?

I'm halfway down the path before Ines' warning echoes clearly in my mind. *The house. The terrace. The courtyard.*

My excitement dies, rendering me frozen mid-step, my eyes on that dirt road. This must be the last of those realms he's restricted me to. In a sense, I think it was his cruelest punishment, more so than the whip. Taunt me with the illusion of freedom and yank it just beyond my reach.

I could always test him, but I'm sure he has a trap ready to be sprung.

The despair that hits me next is so thick, I choke on it. Like always, my first impulse is to give in to fear. Run. Hide. Try to find a drug to dull it and a nice enough outfit to distract from the state of my life. Within Papa's rules, of course. Always within his rules. But he isn't here now…

Somehow, it sinks in at this moment that he's gone. For the first time in my life, Roy Pavalos isn't breathing down my neck or just a phone call away. He isn't here to tell me exactly what to do and how to do it. Though I think this would present a challenge, even for him.

Unless he was in on it.

Yes, my smart, calculating father would suspect from the start that his bodyguard was untrustworthy. He would have always been one step ahead, one move away from declaring checkmate. My kidnapping would only be a mere cog in his wheel, a necessary evil to reach his ultimate goal. I don't think he'd dare to risk my life, though. He needs me too much.

So he'd only put this plan into motion knowing from the outset that Domino would never kill me.

But as I try to cling to this imaginary Papa's scheming, my mind goes blank whenever I come to a motive. He always had a reason. He always let me in on his plan.

Like with Pia.

She's a dangerous little bitch, Ada. That girl is not your friend. What else does she have to do to prove that to you? If you love me, and if you love this family, you'll...

"Lunch is served, Miss."

I whirl around to find Ines standing framed in the doorway to the house. She doesn't look alarmed by how close I am to the limits of the property. With a wave of her hand, she beckons me inside.

I choke down any remaining tears and swipe at what little paint my cheeks.

When I finally return to the house, Ines is waiting for me in that circular room.

"You can eat in your bedroom, Miss," she explains. "Mr. Domino will be home for dinner later this evening. It will be served in the dining room."

With a respectful nod, she heads for the terrace entrance.

My stomach lurches as I creep toward the bedroom, sniffing the air. My "lunch" has been served on the same white table as dinner, this time with just enough for one. A creamy liquid in a glass bowl looks like some kind of soup, paired with another salad and fresh rolls.

I test a drop of the liquid on the tip of my finger and shiver. For all I know, it could be a purée of something far beyond the consistency of most soup ingredients. Like Mama?

I cringe at the thought and back away so suddenly I nearly trip. Turning on my heel, I re-enter the hall, this time venturing back down the end of the corridor opposite the circular foyer.

I assume it curves around the front of the house. There aren't as many windows to break up the pristine white walls. What few I pass reveal snippets of plain, manicured fields, the sky, and a sliver of demarcation in the distance where the lush landscape turns tan. Even so, it must sprawl for miles. Plenty of land to hold a woman captive for only God knows how long.

I think the only way I can still stay sane is to cling to the pathetic fantasy I dreamt up earlier. That Papa is alive, using Domino as a pawn, and my capture was all for a reason. Though what?

Focus, he would command were he here. I can picture him, his stern features set in a hard mask of determination, the eyes we share blazing with the full calculating intelligence that saw him rise from a poor boy living in a *barrio* in Mexico to the dominating force he's become.

Success isn't owed to any man, he told me once. It's bled for. Fought. Won. Those who hesitate wind up at the bottom of the heap. Or worse—they wind up dead.

Always keep your focus, Ada. What we've done, we've done for the family. For the name Pavalos. Never forget that.

As if I ever could. His sin is poison, haunting me for over a decade, consuming my life so that nothing I did could ever free me from his shadow. I think a smart, battered, traumatized woman like the cliché my therapist assumed I fit would see his death as a godsend. Despite how little I have left to live, at least—for once—I'm freed from Roy Pavalos, whatever that means. A part of me wants to believe that it should mean all of my past trauma is miraculously healed and I can proudly take the reins of my own life for the first time ever.

I'm not so naïve. In my father's absence, an even worse monster will rise to take his place. Could Domino Valenciaga be that man?

It kills me to admit that he could. To play the dutiful role of a bodyguard for so long… Five years of lying and scheming. In a twisted way, my father would have been proud.

As much as he seems to hate him, Domino must have picked up many tricks from his Don Roy. A preference of décor, at least, was not one of them.

This house is so plain. Most of the rooms I pass in this section are empty or barely furnished. I doubt this is where he lives. Though, I know for a fact that it isn't. At least not recently.

The Domino I knew dwelled on my father's estate in a converted guesthouse that faced the tennis courts, a good ten-minute walk from the main house—and if you went at night, you'd need a flashlight to cut through the rose gardens to get there. As I did, far too many times to count.

A sound in between a laugh and a sob rips from my throat as I sway, forced to brace my shoulder against the nearest wall to stay standing. Crippling shame washes over me as I recall every time I snuck out at night to see Domino—never with his knowledge or consent, of course. I'd hide behind one of the massive trees lining that section of the property, and I'd watch him.

For hours, I'd watch him.

He paced at night, usually in the small lawn outside his door in that sliver of time after midnight and before dawn once Papa went to bed. He'd pace and pace, with a cigarette in his mouth, and sometimes he'd pause mid-stride and tilt his head back to look up at the sky. He'd take off the hat, setting it at his feet, and rake his free hand through that thick mane of black hair.

I always found something beautiful in those brief, unguarded moments. A realness so different from the cultured façade of perfection I was used to. Curiosity alone kept driving me back there night after night, no matter the weather. Just to watch him.

Some nights, he'd sit in an old lawn chair Mama had relegated to the guesthouse, along with all of the old furniture she no longer deemed worthy of the mansion. He'd cradle a beer on his lap and stare out into the night with a look of such serious devotion on his face. As though whatever troubled his mind required his full focus and concentration. It worried him.

Back then, I assumed it was a woman. I used to seethe over the image of this fictional creature and what she must look like to entice a man like him. The opposite of me, I was sure. A brunette with dark eyes, quiet beauty, and a business degree, perhaps. Someone with her own life far beyond her father's empire. A woman I could never be.

Now I know what truly bothered him all those nights. Me —but not in the way I used to crave he would view me. No, he plotted on how to hurt me. How to hurt my father and my family.

Again, the why feels more pressing than ever to discover. What secrets has Domino Valenciaga been hiding all along? It's funny how, despite all that time I spent watching him, I barely know the first thing about the man.

Apart from my father's story about being rescued by a man from a barrio, I don't even know where he came from. He spent most of his time either by my father's side or in the guesthouse—apart from the few nights he had off when he'd leave the property in a battered blue truck that sputtered so badly I could hear it from my room in the mansion.

Blinking, I refocus on the present and keep moving, inspecting this winding hall with a different focus. He has to sleep somewhere.

Not this room a few paces from where I was standing. Further? I keep going, testing doors as I go. Near the very end of the corridor, I find a room with its door ajar. Cautiously I push it open, peering into what I can clearly recognize as a bedroom. Unlike the one I've woken in, this one sports dark wooden floors and an even larger four-poster bed in a matching shade. The sheets are gray, but overall, the layout of the room is the same. A bed. A mirror that I assume leads to another closet.

One step over the threshold, and I know instantly that I've found it. The place where Domino sleeps, at least while he's held me captive. His stench infects the walls, emanating from the bed itself. He slept here, I bet. Perhaps as recently as last night. He came here and climbed onto those sheets, sleeping soundly after brutalizing me.

The thought disgusts me. Though why am I edging forward? My steps are slow and hesitant. With every inch I gain, I lick my lips, tasting the blood still drying there from his blow. The man is a sick monster who claims to have killed my family.

I shouldn't be so fascinated by the sight of one space I've never glimpsed despite all my years of watching him. I've never been allowed into the guesthouse after he claimed it. I could only watch from afar, and the one corner of the structure where I suspect he slept always had the blinds drawn closed over the windows. Some nights I managed to see the hint of orange light peeking from beneath the barrier. A handful of times, I even caught his shadow moving. Pausing. Undressing in a blur of motion.

I've never glimpsed up close any space wherein he might have let down his guard and ceased being my father's dutiful bodyguard.

Though, perhaps I'm not being entirely truthful. I did see him drop his guard once before…

The memory is so fleeting on its face—a mere fragment of images and few snippets of dialogue. I'm ashamed to have clung to it so fiercely all along. Reliving it now just sows a wave of more confusion. My past admiration of him seems more like a violation in this context. He went out of his way to gain my trust.

And yet he always hated me, I think. He had to—because I would have willingly given him so much more. It sickens me to admit as much, but it's the truth. All he had to do was look at me. Ask. Snap his fingers.

I would have been his. Willingly, I would have been his. I wanted him in a way I've wanted few men in my life…

No. I wanted him more than anyone. I craved him so badly that I'd lie in my bed at night and imagine him, using my fingers to fill in where imagination alone couldn't. I could orgasm just thinking of his eyes. His voice. My only saving grace is that I wasn't enthralled by his looks alone. I had every reason in the world to obsess over Domino Valenciaga—no one could blame me.

Because he saved me once. Thinking back to that moment makes my head throb. I'm remembering it wrong, seeing care and concern in those broad features where none existed. But no…

I remember it clearly, despite how scattered those memories may be. Domino saved my life. He looked at me in a way no one ever had. Not my parents. Not Tristan. Not Pia.

I'd been so drunk, drunker than I'd ever been. Drunk enough to disobey my father and leave the property alone after nightfall.

I only remember walking. For miles and miles, with no real goal in mind. I'd been crying. Crying so hard, my eyes ached and felt swollen; my vision blurred. Eventually, I stumbled across the main road, and I just laid there, right in the middle of the asphalt. It felt so warm, baked by one of the hottest days on record. It was so dark on that stretch of the highway I could barely see my hand in front of my face.

As drunk—and high—as I was, I knew that no one could see me, and I waited. I waited for the pain to stop and the sound of a running engine, and the sight of headlights.

When an amber glow finally washed over me, I smiled. *Finally. Thank you, God,* I whispered to no one.

No longer would I be forced to play pretend. No longer would I have to live as Ada-Maria Lucia Pavalos.

But then I heard a sound I wasn't expecting.

"Ada-Maria!" His voice bellowed out like thunder, richer than I'd ever heard it. I'd been so high, I assumed it was God, at first, responding to my plea. Then I saw him in human form, kneeling over me, more beautiful than any natural-born man had a right to be. Domino…

"What the hell is wrong with you?" he demanded, wrenching me by my shoulders into a sitting position. He shook me, making my head loll back and forth, all while shouting. "You stupid spoiled little bitch! Have you lost your fucking mind? You trying to kill yourself?"

I think I still hadn't come to terms with the fact that he found me, assuming he was merely a specter conjured by my addled brain.

"Yes," I told him. "I want to die. Just let me go."

I asked him so nicely. As though it was a favor I needed him to do for me.

Then I saw the anger wash over his face. Looking back, I can clearly denote the fractures in his carefully constructed mask. I should have seen the truth then. But in that moment, I remember being startled from my daze as if struck by lightning.

He looked so furious at the thought of me dying. Furious and pained and so damn sexy, I would have done whatever he asked me to. Whatever he wanted.

All he did was drag me from the road and shove me into the back of his truck.

"You stupid little—" He broke off, clearing his throat. "I'm taking you home now, Ms. Ada-Maria," he added in his usual, cold tone.

I'd been so dazed by the whiplash that it wasn't until the following night—when my sober brain could piece together how I'd gotten home—that I realized it wasn't a dream. He saved me.

Then he ignored me the next morning as though nothing happened. He never told Papa either, from what I could garner without asking directly.

I never complained to Papa about the way he spoke to me, either. *You spoiled little bitch.* I used to replay those words to myself—usually when I had two fingers inside of me and needed one last hit to go over the edge. I'd think of him snarling those hateful words, and I'd orgasm, gasping his name softly enough that no one ever knew.

He treated me a way no one ever had. I'd been stupid enough to think that meant something. That I meant something to *someone.*

And now I know.

Domino saved my life that night because he had a more gruesome death in mind. Those things he said to me weren't the impassioned speech of someone afraid for my life. They were the frustrations of my would-be murderer.

And God, I wish he never found me, then. It's been two years since, and I've never gathered up the strength to try again. Maybe I stopped hating myself.

Or perhaps I knew, deep down, that Domino might not be there to stop me the next time.

CHAPTER NINE

My back hurts so goddamn much. I cry out, waking up to a darkened room, already on the verge of tears. At first, I assume I'm in that pretty white prison.

But wait…

This smell is different, so rich I audibly groan at the flavor, inhaling deeply to savor it. Then I remember. I'm in Domino's room, on his bed.

Alarmed, I bolt upright, disentangling myself from his sheets.

Because, sometime during my reminiscence of the past, I climbed onto the mattress beneath them. I lied in the same space as the man who tormented me, and, worst of all, I fell asleep breathing in the remnants of him.

I'd vomit if there were anything in my stomach left to bring up.

Instead, I lurch to my feet, scanning the room warily, expecting to find him stepping from the shadows. It's nearly evening now, I realize with a start. Beyond the windows, the sun has partially sunk beneath the horizon. I've lost hours.

And he'll be back soon.

Knowledge of that spurs me toward the doorway. I need to hide. Prepare. Do something other than wait for him patiently. I should devise a trap.

My father would. Usually, I would play a part in it. Domino mentioned the day I interrupted my father's meeting with the mayor—but I don't think he knew what happened after I entered that room. I sidled up to the man with a charming smile and playfully mentioned that I'd like a ride in the sports car he had parked outside. Of course, he gave me a ride hours later in that very car and fucked me in the back seat.

And while he wasn't looking, I slipped a vial of cocaine in the glove box.

What secrets does Domino have waiting to be found? Everyone has them, skeletons in their closet. Figuratively. Literally…

My heart pounds as I turn on the threshold and cross over to the full-length mirror directly opposite the bed. Copying Ines' motions, I feel along the edge until I find a concealed latch. Once I press it, the door easily swings inward, revealing a closet twice as large as the one in my room.

One look, and I realize that if Domino has any secrets hidden within his house, they might be within here. There's luggage, for one. I spy it lurking on a top shelf.

Another glaring sight is just how few items of clothing hang on the rails. I count maybe three suits, a handful of dress shirts, and even fewer slacks. A lone pair of leather shoes fills only one rung in a shelf that seems built to hold at least fifty. I only find one red tie.

But this closet contains one fixture mine didn't. In the center is a square, glass-topped counter. Beneath it, arranged neatly within separate wooden boxes lined with black silk, are watches. So many watches. I count at least forty different kinds. Most of them are stopwatches. Some gold, or silver. If I strain my ears, a strange ticking sound echoes faintly. They're all working, counting down the seconds.

I wonder if Ines' constant reminders about the time were more than just a devoted need to adhere to her boss' wishes. Of course, they weren't. She was being timed.

I was being timed.

Anger flares, as sharp as it is irrational. Perhaps he got a kick out of being the one to call the shots instead of the lackey taking orders. Though, come to think of it, I never saw my father order him outright the way he did everyone else— myself included. When it came to Domino, he seemed to adhere to a different code. I think it might have been respect.

And this is how he was betrayed.

I shake my head to clear it. *No.* I can't focus on the past any longer. The only hope I have of staying alive is to think, plot, plan.

I scan the room again with a different focus, hunting in the corners and behind the hanging clothing. There must be something. Some clue. Some bit of information he forgot to hide.

I'm nearing the back of the room when I finally spy something tucked behind a rack of shelves—a duffle bag made of black leather, like the kind someone might carry onto a plane. The main interior is empty, but when I open the zipper of one of the side compartments, a wealth of different materials spills out.

I crouch to retrieve them, feeling my hands shake as I realize what they are. Pictures. Some are grainy, like paparazzi shots taken from afar, barely in focus. Others are crystal clear, taken up close with the subject's full awareness.

I lift the nearest one, straining my eyes to make out the details.

"Son of a bitch."

It's Tristan. His back is to the camera, but I recognize his signature navy suit and the red imported sports car he loved to show off. That car was the only reason I gave him the time of day.

That and the fact that I had no choice.

I grapple for another picture that must have been taken soon after. It shows a passenger leaving the same vehicle, a woman in a tiny black dress. The one lying next to it shows her face, her bitchy grin visible even from the distance she stood from the photographer.

Alexi Rojas.

Is it fair to feel jealous over a man I truly never loved in the first place? *Yes,* I decide. Though, the fact that Tristan isn't here to bitch at helps temper my rage. I just feel hollow. Used. Lied to—a time stamp above each photo reveals the date of this particular meeting.

Just a week ago.

Another set of images were taken just a few days later, shot from a different angle inside the hallway of what looks like Tristan's apartment complex. In one, Alexi is visible sauntering up to his door at nine p.m. She doesn't leave until six a.m. the next morning.

At least five different instances are depicted in the photos altogether, spanning from a month ago up to just two days before our date at the restaurant. I'm sure he was with her that night as well.

And apparently, he wasn't the only one fucking her.

Four photos remain, each one a glossier, higher-quality shot from the others. These were taken up close and personal —*very* personal. If I didn't know Tristan's body so well, I'd assume it was him.

His hand, fondling the perky breast of a smirking blond. His fingers gripping her hair to expose her neck and the tiny heart tattoo on her collar bone.

Objectively, at least I know now why Tristan enjoyed fucking her so much that even the allure of dating Roy Pavalos' daughter wasn't enough to temper the lust. She's hot, with flawless skin and a taut little ass, and I hate her so goddamn much I could scream.

Tristan, she could have—the bastard could barely last seven minutes in the sack on a good day.

But I recognize those hands. That tanned, golden skin. The coiled, rigid muscle shaping his forearms…

For all of his taunts and superiority displayed toward me, Domino had no problem fucking a "worthless whore" like Alexi Rojas.

I think a part of me wants to laugh, almost as much as I want to seethe. For all intents and purposes, Alexi and I are one and the same—though hell, I think I have more than two brain cells to rub together, so maybe that's it. Domino likes his women flawless and stupid.

It fits.

Or maybe he just likes his women so easy they'd give it to anyone like a cat in heat?

Disgusted, I start to shove the photos back into the duffle only to jar something else loose. I almost missed it, hidden at the very bottom of the pocket. Two items, actually. One is a brown vial of liquid. It looks medical, like something taken from a hospital or doctor's office. Printed on a white label is the phrasing—*LORAZEPAM 2mg/ml injection solution.* Ativan, a drug I know well enough, thanks to my mother. She kept a pill bottle of it in the medicine cabinet. Her prescription was for one milligram as needed. She took three.

A chilling sensation washes over me as I realize that this might be what he drugged me with. How much? And for how long?

A shudder runs through me as I brush my hand across my sore thigh. Perhaps that's where they did it?

Beside the vial, is a syringe with a needle attached, still packaged for use.

A plan forms in my brain as reckless as it is desperate. It could work. I ignore the many cons and focus on the slim possibility of success.

Without thinking it through, I shove the pictures back into the pocket and return the duffle behind the shelf. Then I escape his room and return to mine.

My heart pounds as I glance over my shoulder with every noise to break the quiet. How soon before he comes back? What if he's already here?

I strain my ears, listening for any telltale sign. All I hear are chirping birds and murmuring insects. Apart from its purpose as my prison, more and more, the abject beauty of this landscape sticks out to me—as well as the fact that it's far from Terra Rodea.

There are none of the hallmarks of the city or its outskirts. The land beyond this lush estate looks dead. Like desert.

The nearest area with remotely similar terrain is hours from the city at least. I eye the vial in my hand and wonder how much he had shoved into my body just to bring me here. It was night at the restaurant and night by the time I came to in the foyer. I'd blurred them together, assuming they happened hours apart, but what if they were two different nights?

Which means that he was ready for me. The grill. The dress. He waited for my arrival and used every second since to torment me.

For what? Something tells me that there has to be a reason behind the madness. I guess I'm not insane enough to see it. My head aches again, the room spinning.

Then footsteps echo in the distance, advancing quickly in this direction.

Damn! I lunge for the closet. At the last minute, I pivot toward the bed and shove the vial and syringe beneath the top corner of the mattress.

I've barely stepped back from it when a shadow appears at the door.

"Mr. Domino is ready for you in the dining room, Miss," Ines calls.

My heart drops to the floor, and I almost can't disguise my alarm.

Domino is already here. For how long?

Long enough to see me creep through his belongings, laughing all the while in the background?

"He requests that you not change," Ines adds, and I jump to realize she's still here. "You can follow me."

A not-so-subtle warning not to delay.

"Y-Yes." I smooth my hand along the front of the dress. It's rumpled now, and I'm sure my hair is a rat's nest. I can't stop myself from combing my fingers through it as I hurry into the hall.

Again, the house transforms in the warm glow of sunset. This time, the fiery hue painting the walls resembles less of a figurative hell and more like a literal fire, threatening to consume me with greedy, grasping flames.

CHAPTER TEN

I smell him, even before we near the doorway to the dining room.

Domino.

He's seated at the head of the table again, his hands folded in front of him. He's switched the white shirt for one of gray, and somehow this color unnerves me the most. Perhaps because it acts as a neutral tone, softening the intensity of his eyes while enhancing the hardness of his features.

"Have a seat, Ada-Maria," he says, gesturing to the chair nearest him. "I promise that tonight, only chicken is on the menu."

I stiffen. "Not *Pollo d-de Roy?*" My voice breaks so badly I can barely get the words out. Tears fall, lashing down my cheeks but I don't dare wipe them away. I should crave any and every reminder of what he's done.

What he's claimed to have done, anyway.

"No, that is not on the menu tonight," Domino says, tilting his head to observe me. "I hope you enjoyed your full day to yourself. It will be the last you may have for a while."

I grit my teeth, alarmed by just how easily the threat creeps into his voice. I suspect he chooses now to deploy that bit of information for a reason. Most likely as a prompt to get me to ask, "Are… Are you going to kill me?"

He laughs. "Have a seat, Ada-Maria. This time, I'm afraid, the meal isn't entirely for your benefit. I'm starving."

Surprisingly, I sense a note of truthfulness in his voice. Maybe shock alone is what finally draws me closer to the table. I pick a chair halfway down the table from him, but as I pull it out, he shakes his head.

"No. No games tonight; you sit by me."

I bite back a sigh and approach him, still smoothing my hands down my front. God, it's as if every little thing I do might give away what I've done if I'm not careful. My hands shake. I don't know what to do with them. Can he somehow sense traces of the drug vial on them?

He says nothing as I sit. Here, his scent hits me full in the face, and another thought creeps in before I can help it, far beyond escape or my kidnapping.

I wonder how he smelled after fucking Alexi, drenched in her cheap perfume. The two-dollar hooker smell wouldn't mesh well with the spicy tinge of his aftershave. Though hell, they deserved each other. Why should it matter?

Still, sometimes I wonder if Tristan thought I really was as dumb as I looked, or if he just didn't care to hide it. He never tried to wash her smell off him. I was paranoid that I could taste her on his lips whenever he kissed me.

My only saving grace had been to remind myself that Tristan was too selfish a lover to go down on me, let alone her. But who knows? It kills me that I don't.

And now Domino…

"You seem distracted tonight, Ada-Maria."

He's touching me—a reality that doesn't sink in until I see his fingers moving from the corner of my eye, twisting a strand of my hair around a thick, calloused thumb.

"Tell me you've been a good girl while I was gone." His inflection dips in a way that makes me shiver. He wants an answer.

"I-I did what you said I could do." Belatedly, I realize how pathetic that sounded. Weak.

But as sick as it is to admit, I think I satisfied him. His tongue flits across his lower lip.

"*Only* what I said? You wouldn't lie to me, now would you, Ada-Maria?"

I jump, nearly choking on the nerves bouncing beneath my skin. The only way to distract from them is to speak, so I blurt the first thing that comes to mind. "You know a lot about lying, don't you?"

He sits back and claps his hands, ushering in another parade of servers who place a series of platters onto the table. At least he wasn't lying. The platters of baked meat look and smell like seasoned chicken, though I barely pay attention to them, or any of the other dishes.

For whatever reason, something makes me meet his gaze and hold it.

"I never lied to you," I say.

He sits forward again, leaning his face alarmingly close to mine. "Your father did plenty of lying for the both of us," he says. Reaching past me, he drags a plate so close to the table's edge it nearly falls into my lap. "Eat. Help yourself."

One of his servants fills his plate before scurrying out of sight.

I don't touch mine.

"I never lied to you." It feels important to repeat that. To ensure he can hear the honesty in my voice. And the hate.

"No…" He lifts a glass of wine I didn't notice until then. Bringing the rim to his mouth, he inspects me before taking a slow sip. "You just lied to everyone else, didn't you? Though considering the family you grew up in, do you even know what's the lie and what isn't?"

I hate how damn smug he sounds. I reach for my own drink only to stop short inches before bringing it to my lips, sloshing wine onto my lap.

"It's not poisoned," he admits—grudgingly, I suspect. His reluctance alone gives me the courage to take a sip.

It's divine. One of the finest vintages I've ever tasted, and I nearly choke in my rush to gulp it down.

"Didn't your Papa teach you, Ada-Maria? Never drink on an empty stomach."

Gasping for air, I sloppily set my glass aside, relishing the soothing burn of alcohol. It alone must give me the courage to spar verbally with him.

"My father taught me that all men are bastards who lie, and cheat, and steal. It's good to see that he, at least, didn't lie to me." It's a selective way of looking at it.

One he isn't amused by.

"Lie to you... Like your Tristan?"

I flinch, feeling fear flood my veins. Does he know that I found the pictures? Or was I so stupid as to give myself away? I can't tell.

Peeling his gaze from mine, he turns his focus to his food.

"You should eat." He picks up a fork and stabs at a piece of meat. Then he palms a knife and slowly severs it into pieces.

I swallow hard, flicking my gaze toward the selection of silverware lying beside my place setting. I wasn't given a knife, just a fork, and spoon.

"Miguel is a damn good cook who excels at preparing both impeccable entrees as well as corrupt politicians. Don't hold one experience against him. Eat."

"You make a joke out of it?" I croak hoarsely. "Cooking my father like some fucking animal?"

He inclines his head and samples a bite of meat. "You and I both know that he's done far worse to far more people, Ada-Maria."

Do I know that?

"N-No," I insist, pushing back from the table. "He could be ruthless, but even he wasn't that cruel—"

"Did he whip you?"

His tone startles me more than the question itself. I would never expect that low, gruff note. Like he cares. Does he?

No, I decide, looking at him. He merely wants another way to get inside my head.

"*You* did," I point out.

"Yes." He stabs at a green vegetable and brings it to his mouth. "I did. Which reminds me..." He pushes back from the table as well and motions with his hand. "Stand up."

My first impulse is to immediately sink into my chair.

His eyes take on that hard gleam again. He isn't asking. "I said stand up—"

I nearly knock over my chair in my haste to comply. When I do, he jerks his chin, and I step back from the table.

"Turn around."

My cheeks flame as I spin. When his low growl catches my ears, I go rigid.

"Goddamn," he rasps.

I don't know why I look. Something well beyond fear compels me to. When I glance over my shoulder, I find him stroking his jaw, his eyes on my sore, rent skin. Only by watching him do I catch his lips move and make sense of the rough grumble of syllables to leave his mouth next.

"So fucking beautiful."

Beautiful. Only a monster would find beauty in blood and pain. Whatever drug he gave me has long since worn off. I can feel every stinging, burning inch, and it hurts. But when I delve into that pain, my wounds don't seem to be the source of it. Just a selfish, vain realization.

He finds me beautiful only like this, bloodied and broken.

But he fucked Alexi with her perfect flawless skin. He didn't have to whip her.

"I always knew there was something wrong with you." The words are flying off my tongue, and it's too late to choke them back. I blame the wine.

From his amused glance, I assume he does as well.

"You did, did you?" He returns to the table and pours himself a serving of wine. Then he reaches for my glass and fills it as well. "Is that what you were thinking every time you pranced before me in one of those tight ass little skirts? That I was *wrong* for you?"

I grit my teeth. "I could have anyone in Terra Rodea," I snap.

He nods and takes a slow sip of wine. "Anyone but me."

He's right.

I think of him again with Alexi. Fucking that bitch.

Impulsively, I stagger to the table, snatching my glass of wine. I start to bring it to my mouth but sometime during the motion, I pivot and hurl it against the wall instead.

It shatters, and the liquid goes flying, staining the white wall like blood.

"You'll wish you hadn't done that," Domino warns.

Pride is a strong enough barrier against fear. "If I wanted you, I could have had you," I tell him. "You think you're better than any other sycophant to circle around my father like a vulture? You're all the same, with the same greedy cock and the same taste for a tiny waist and big tits. In fact, you were never worth my time—"

I don't even see him move.

My chin is in his grasp before I know it, wrenched back until I have no choice but to meet his gaze.

"And if I wanted you, I would have had you dripping wet any time of day and anywhere, wouldn't I, Ada-Maria? God, you couldn't hide it even if you tried. I only had to snap my fingers, and you'd suck my cock in a heartbeat, wouldn't you? Even in the bath…"

He trails off, but my brain picks up the sordid taunt for him. When he touched me, I reacted the exact opposite way a woman should respond to her captor. With insatiable need, like a shameless whore.

Stab. I want to stab him with the syringe, injecting every ounce of Ativan. God, I want to. My fingers twitch with the desire, and I wrench out of his grasp, contemplating running to my room and grabbing the vial now. Seizing my chance.

Wait. It takes effort to choke down the shame and rage and find the tendril of logic lurking beneath. I can't be stupid and waste my only chance at escape. A better route would be to milk him for whatever I can and lure him into relaxing his guard.

"You were always so transparent, Ada-Maria," Domino taunts, drawing my notice again. I wonder if he's been speaking to me all this time. "So desperate. So fucking pathetic—"

"Then what do you want with me, then?" I try not to let the pain in my voice show.

I fail.

Regardless, I turn to him, meeting those cold green eyes once more.

"Why kill my father but take me?"

"Why?" He laughs and snags my chin again. Using it as an anchor, he drags me toward him, bringing our faces within an inch of each other's. "I want something from you, Ada-Maria. Something that your father entrusted into your pathetic, weak little brain. I want you to be honest with me. Where is the Inglecias file?"

I rip out of his grasp. "Don't touch me—"

"Then answer me." He advances a step, his expression colder than ever. "Where is the fucking file?"

"I don't know what you're talking about!"

"God damnit..." He's closer in an instant, pressing his thumb against my bottom lip so hard it clips against my teeth. "You're stupid, Ada, but not that stupid. Though sometimes, I will admit. You have me fooled."

His voice... It's dangerous, rumbling through my belly. So deep. So hoarse.

The way I'd imagine him sounding during sex, too drunk on lust to give a damn about maintaining his ruse as a stoic bodyguard.

Enough! I shake my head to snap out of it. It's the damn wine addling my senses. Nothing more.

But then why is he frowning, still stroking my lip. Over and over again. "Give me what I want," he tells me, contorting his voice into a mockery of gentleness. The effect is more alarming than when he shouts. "Be a good girl, and I'll make this easier on you. Though admittedly, your fate is already far beyond my hands, Ada-Maria—"

"Get off me!"

I strike his chest with the flat of my hand and stagger away from him, crashing into the table as a result. Without looking, I feel along the polished surface for a weapon. Something. Anything. Then, as if by a miracle, my finger catches the edge of something sharp. Alarmingly sharp.

I find a dull surface to grab and brandish my weapon before me.

"Leave me alone."

Rather than cower in alarm, he laughs. "You couldn't use that on me even if you wanted to. Here, I'll help." In two strides, he's practically on top of me, snatching my wrist— but rather than wrench the knife away, he manipulates my grasp until I'm holding the tip against his throat.

"Go on and do it, Ada-Maria," he goads. "If you go straight into the artery, it's easy. There will be no resistance from any muscle or bone—at first. Until the full extent of the bleeding kicks in. I hope you like a nice, hot shower because that's what it will feel like—" his voice softens, damn near a whisper. "A warm, relaxing shower that tastes like salt and will stain that pretty little dress. So do it. I'll even get it started for you..."

Horrified, I watch as he tightens his grip, driving the tip of the blade into his skin. He bleeds in a fat bead of scarlet that wells up right over the edge of the knife.

"N-No!" I pull back, and he lets me go. Off-balance, I stagger back and trip, landing on my knees.

"Thought so." He shrugs, knife in hand, and brushes his thumb along the small nick on his neck. "A damn shame —" he brings that finger to his mouth and licks the tip. "I was looking forward to it. Your body covered in blood has always been a fantasy of mine."

I choke. At the back of my mind, I realize this is exactly what he wants—to push me to the brink. I'm playing right into his hands by shivering, gaping in fear.

My father operated the same way. Men like them rule by terror. The ability to sow confusion and doubt in their enemies so that they never see the knife poised to stab them in the back. I can't resist glancing over my shoulder just in case.

"I'll warn you, Ada-Maria," Domino says. "I'm almost bored of our game. Give me something useful if you want to play a little longer. Inglecias. Where did the bastard keep the file?"

I truly don't know, but I sense that now isn't the time to admit that. Instead, I ask the obvious question and pray it doesn't set him off. "Why do you care?"

He blinks, his eyes narrowing. "Information is money," he says, switching back to that disarming growl. "Let's just say I know someone willing to pay a damn lot for said information. Where is the Inglecias file—"

"It's personal to you, isn't it?" I ask, seeing through the lie. Still, I'm not completely sure I'm right until a muscle in his jaw lurches angrily.

"Where is it?"

"Did you know Pia?"

How could he, though?

We knew everything there was to know about each other. Or at least, we *did*. Weeks before she went missing, my charming, chatty friend grew quiet and evasive about what she did in her free time. And with whom.

I do have my own life, you realize? she sniped at me once, too busy eying a delicate silver ring on her left hand to even look at me.

Soon, she wasn't just keeping secrets. Our meetings after school became shorter and more infrequent, but she wasn't in any extracurriculars to explain all those consumed hours. I even asked her once, if she were seeing a boy.

Her response was a sly smirk and a wink. *I could be, though I wouldn't call him a boy. Why, Adie? Are you jealous?*

Of course, I was, and out of sheer pride, I never asked her again. Domino is in his early thirties now, meaning he would have been in his twenties back then. Too old? For a normal teenager, perhaps, but I soon learned that Pia's taste skewed far older than that.

Which makes Domino a fitting candidate, nonetheless.

"Congratulations, Ada-Maria," Domino says dryly. "You have managed to bore me—"

"Have I?" A dangerous stunt comes to mind. It's stupid, but I have nothing left to lose. He claims to not care? Then he can prove it. I wet my lips with the tip of my tongue and say, "Pia Inglecias was a stupid, dumb bitch, and she deserved whatever the hell she got."

He lunges, his eyes flashing. I don't think he even realizes what he's done until his hand is already around my throat, snatching the chain and pulling so tight my eyes bulge.

"How dare you even talk about her?"

"So you knew her," I croak, my eyes watering.

He lets me go as I grapple with the fact that I managed to pry some sliver of information loose from him. He couldn't fake that kind of anger. He knew Pia.

And that irrational sense of jealousy returns. I am ten times better than Alexi Rojas in every goddamn way. But Pia? She was always the brighter star of our trio, shining so fiercely I was all but invisible in her shadow.

But back then, I didn't mind being invisible. As the stereotypical ugly fat friend, I think I was at my happiest. I could live as Ada without being seen as my father's tool or a hot piece of ass. In so many ways, it was a better existence than having to stand on my own. Even forty pounds lighter, with a full face of makeup, I always knew at the back of my mind that if Pia were still here, I wouldn't come close.

Domino loving her…*that* I could understand.

"If you knew her," I croak, rubbing at my throat, "then you probably have a better idea of what happened to her than I do, or my father. She was barely talking to me when she left."

A fact that my father used to his advantage. *Why show loyalty to someone who only ever used you?* he demanded. *I am the only one who will ever protect you. Go do this for me…*

"And even now, you continue to play dumb," Domino hisses. The level of disgust in his voice stings. Almost as much as his anger confuses me. "Pia Inglecias is dead," he says. "Don't look so fucking surprised. I'm sure you know when, where, and have been dancing on her grave for the past ten years. Your father kept meticulous records concerning all of that, I'm sure. How he blackmailed the Inglecias family and tried to have them killed—"

"Pia… She's not dead." I can barely say those words out loud. I haven't, not once since she's been missing—even if I've suspected as much in the pit of my soul. She can't be dead. She ran away because she bit off more than she could chew. As for blackmail…

My father wouldn't waste time trying to threaten anyone to keep them silent. He'd cover his tracks too well to care.

"She ran away," I say slowly. I could laugh at the expression on his face. Or scream. "If you were fucking her back then, you'd know that—"

"Pia is dead." His voice rings out, chillingly final. "Stop with the little girl lost act. Your father killed her. You know that—"

"No." I shake my head. "No, he wouldn't."

"And how can you be so fucking sure of that? He's killed women before. Children—"

"No!" I stagger to my feet. "He wouldn't kill Pia, because I had to make *sure* he wouldn't. I'm sure he gave her some money and made her skip town—"

"What do you mean?" He sounds so hoarse. So desperate that I almost forget the monster I'm speaking to.

"Pia stole from us," I say, gutted by the admission years later.

My nearest and dearest friend turned out to be like everyone else in my shitty life—interested in me only as far as my last name went.

"She used me to break into my father's private office, and she took money from the safe. A lot of money. My father was so pissed…" I shiver at the thought, feeling the marks on my back prickle. Not the new ones—the older ones that may have superficially healed, but they always cut deeper than my skin. "He told me that he didn't want to press charges. He just wanted her to know how it felt to have someone steal something important. So, I snuck into her room and took her diary. He was going to use it as leverage to make her return the money."

In retrospect, it was just a stupid act, too petty to despair over. In reality, I was saving Pia from a hell of a lot worse. But still, I never felt dirtier than I did then.

Until I read said journal, of course, and felt even worse…

"I'm sure he gave her some of the money," I blurt, aware of Domino waiting. "And she skipped town, too ashamed to show her face."

"She's dead." Something in his voice makes me look at him again. His eyes are glazed, his lips set in a firm line that makes me suspect that he's moved beyond anger. He's suspicious. And confused.

"I wouldn't lie about something like that."

"No," he admits, and I'm startled by the sigh of relief that rips through me. "You spoiled little fool. Pia didn't steal money from that bastard. She stole—" He breaks off, stopping himself from revealing too much. "Now I know why Roy kept you so fucking close all this time. It wasn't because you were in on his schemes. You were just dumb enough to believe him at every turn. I'm sure that helped him sleep at night."

He isn't joking. He's dead serious.

"Stop talking like you know me! You don't know me!"

"Don't I?" His eyes flash, warning me to tread carefully. "I've known you from that very first day in Don Roy's office, Ada-Maria. I saw you then in crystal-clear focus. A woman with enough beauty to get a man hard in seconds. And the brains of a fucking bunny rabbit. You react to every man the same and prance around, noticing only those with a nice credit card or a sexy sports car—with your Papa's permission, of course. Am I too far off?"

"Yes. You're wrong," I snap.

But he's not.

Fully aware of that, he smirks, his eyes glittering. "How so? The brains part? Or your choice in men? Tell me, in between that lawyer you're fucking and the old man you let screw you a month before dating him, where am I off base?"

My cheeks heat with shame because he's right. I wait for him to grind my nose in my biggest fault of all—wanting him.

"I'm surprised you knew my name, Ada-Maria. At least beyond being your father's dutiful lackey."

And there I have it. It's stupid to cling to this one shred of triumph, but I do.

"I wanted you more than anyone," I blurt, sounding smug for once. "Always."

His smirk falls. "For a viper, bred from a family of liars, you sure are terrible at it."

Though I should be lying. I shouldn't want to prove him wrong. Obviously, this is bait to goad me into the trap of admitting my attraction to him. Still, I can't seem to resist tripping right into it.

"I always wanted you," I tell him, licking my lips as my mouth suddenly goes dry. He doesn't race to cut me off this time. He's watching, waiting. "Always. I watched you every night, in front of the guesthouse. I always tried to speak to you. And when I was in bed alone, I'd—"

I've said too much. My chest is heaving as every breath becomes a struggle. This dress feels too tight. My back is on fire, and beneath his gaze, I've never felt smaller, as fragile as the wine glass lying in pieces across the room.

Because in this moment, at least, all he wants to do is shatter me.

"I am not one of your old men, Ada-Maria," he warns. "Don't play your mind games on me."

A suggestion I am more than willing to heed. I'm so tired. I think of that bed in the room he's made my cell—but not the drugs hidden beneath my mattress. I just want to hide.

"Don't you dare run from me."

I'm spinning on my heel anyway, racing for the door. My thoughts are a blur. I don't even have a clear aim in mind but to run. When I finally make out a direction, I realize that I'm not heading toward that large, rounded door. I'm staggering into that white bedroom instead.

I can hear him behind me, his steps deliberately slow. *Thump. Thump.* They echo as steadily as the ticking of those clocks he has. As relentless and inescapable as time itself.

Think! I move to the bed, gripping the end of the mattress just as he appears in the doorway.

"I think I've grown tired enough of these games, Ada-Maria." He takes a step, and the harsh, pristine backdrop merely serves to illustrate how massive he truly is. So tall, with muscle straining against the sleeves of his shirt. The sliver of his chest visible ripples, his body tense with rage.

Viewing him now, I realize that there is no realistic way I could ever overpower him enough to deliver an injection. My only chance is to get him to relax his guard. To have him sit on the bed of his own accord, or sleep here, even…

One solution suddenly comes to mind—I could seduce him.

And I don't have any other choice.

Any shame or doubt, I push out of my brain as I meet his gaze again. "Why did you never come on to me?" I ask him, fighting to keep my breathing under control.

He laughs, but the question has the effect I want. He's distracted from his anger for now, at least.

He inclines his head, viewing me from behind dangerously thick lashes. Rather than soften his features, the attribute only serves to obscure what little emotion lurks within his gaze. "I thought I was clear enough on that point? No amount of beauty in the world can disguise a soulless interior—"

"I'm not talking about marriage, Domino," I say, sounding stronger than I feel. "I'm talking about sex. I'm sure you've fucked plenty of women with dirty little souls."

Alexi, for one. Knowing he's been with her reveals his high and mighty act for what it is. An act. Which means he had another reason for avoiding me.

"Was it because of my father?" I ask while gathering the nerve to take a step from my hiding place, toward the foot of the bed.

When I do, he narrows his eyes, those beautiful lips parting as if to order me to stop. He doesn't.

So, I creep forward another step. "He isn't here now."

Despite everything, I can't keep my voice from breaking. The reason for my father's absence is standing right here before me while I try to… What?

Seduce him?

If it were possible to, I would have at any other point during the last five years. Perhaps I wasn't desperate enough?

Because I think he likes this. Watching me tremble before him, toeing some invisible line. To cross it would mean debasing myself fully, forfeiting any ounce of self-worth I may have left. Then again, I am a Pavalos.

Nothing trumps survival.

I finger the neckline of my dress. His eyes track the motion, halting my next breath.

"You would fuck me now?" he asks gruffly. "Why? In hopes that I'd be so enamored by that magic pussy I'd let you go?"

I flinch as the jab strikes its target. "N-No. I'm just curious," I whisper. "You haven't tried to touch me."

Not outside of a brutal context, at least.

"If you wanted me, why not?"

"Because the world doesn't revolve around Ada-Maria Pavalos," he snarls, closing the distance between us. "I can die a happy man without fucking you. Trust me on that."

"But you don't have to." The air feels so heavy, every breath takes the utmost effort. Sweat dampens my skin, and I'm aware of how thin this dress is. How sore my back is. How insane it is to play with fire and consider fucking the man who kidnapped me and killed my father.

I've done far worse in my life.

But the flicker of excitement in my belly makes this time so different from the others. I shouldn't *want* this...

"Why not fuck me, if you could?" I ask, my voice heavy. "Especially if you don't plan on letting me go?"

"Because I don't want to be gentle, that's why." He grabs my throat, wrenching me closer before I can react.

I panic, struggling against his grasp before I realize that this is what I wanted. His nostrils flare with my scent as his gaze dips to my breasts.

Startled, I dare to assume that my seduction attempt is *working*.

"I wouldn't be," he says with the sincerity of a promise, still on the topic of gentleness. "I'd fuck you so hard, I'd—" He bites off the rest, but my brain takes up the task of imagining what he'd say. What he'd do to me. *Bite*, I think, given how his lower lip is skewered between his teeth, so hard the flesh is reddened.

Fear rises up, countering the fragile logic I've come up with. I couldn't willingly let someone like him have me. It would be insane. Dangerous.

"That fucking mouth," Domino growls, his eyes on the feature in question. "The things I've imagined those lips doing."

It's like my offer does something to him, unlocking the dangerous confessions I doubt he'd otherwise voice.

"If you want to play, then who am I to stop you?" He grabs my wrist, turning for the door.

To fuck me somewhere *else*, far from my only bit of leverage.

"W-Wait!" There isn't time to think or plan. I lunge for him, pressing my mouth to his, clawing at his shirt to feel the hard planes of his chest beneath.

For a second—just one—I forget. My brain overloads and melts with the sensation I've dreamt about for so long. Few men live up to the hype their good looks and stature imply. Tristan is a prime example. Sex with him was a chore I had to endure, moaning at the right times to keep him excited. I don't think anyone ever exceeded my expectations.

But this…

This is violent. He nips at my lips until they part, stealing his way inside. His taste, his scent, his heat. I'm drunk on all three, dizzy and breathless within seconds.

Abruptly, he pulls away, stepping back, his lips wet. He was toying with me, of course. Just as I think the thought, he snags a handful of my dress, lifting it.

The style forces me to raise my arms to assist him. I swallow in anticipation of his expression as the final piece of fabric is lifted away.

What I find is hunger. Raw open lust so scorching my skin feels seared in the face of it. The restraint he showed in the bath snaps. Boldly, he cups my breast against his palm, groaning at the feel.

I stop breathing at the sensation of his touch. Heavy and rough—yet soft and teasing. He is a wealth of contradictions as he strokes the peak of my nipple with his thumb.

I can't suppress a gasp.

At the sound, his eyes meet mine again, darkening as if he's battling some internal dilemma. Whatever conclusion he reaches makes him shrug.

"Fuck it." That gruff exhale is my only warning as he shoves me back onto the mattress. He rakes his gaze over me, settling between my legs.

At the same time, he's already ripping open the front of his slacks, and my eyes latch onto his movements, more curious than I'd ever admit out loud.

He's gorgeous. He's terrifying.

Already erect, he springs free, and I'm horrified to realize that I don't know what initially aroused him. My offer? Or seeing my back in the dining room?

Without revealing the answer, he steps forward, mounting the bed after me, and my attention returns to the task at hand. Not that he seems inclined to let me take the lead. He shoves my left thigh aside, making room for him to crouch between both. Harsh, his hands slide beneath my hips, yanking me closer.

A thrill shoots down my spine, mingling with a fiery burst of pain. It hurts, but the pain is like a welcome anchor to the grim reality. This isn't about lust, or even fucking.

This is war. To stay alive, I have to grit my teeth and bear the agony. I have to arch my hips into him, choking out a moan the way I have so many times before.

"Don't." A sharper sting overrides the various aches I feel. His nails, gripping the swell of my ass, biting deep. I gasp in shock.

And he pinches me again.

"No faking," he commands. "No pretending. I don't want that shit. I want…"

He doesn't tell me. Instead, he shoves his hand between my legs, sliding what feels like a thumb against my outer lips. I can't silence a cry of alarm. It feels…

Like I imagined it would. So damn good. His skin alone sows devious friction, and I can't stop my legs from drifting further apart, opening myself to more.

But his goal isn't to savor me. He rams a thick finger in deep without warning.

My eyelids flutter. *Holy shit.* He's rough, entering me swiftly without care. Like he's searching for something.

Gravely, his voice rumbles against my ear, revealing exactly what. "Wet." He says it with such disgust. Such awe. It's a marvelous discovery. A trap.

As if to prove the slickness he finds is real, he eases another finger alongside the first, stretching them both. Together. Apart. Further. *Too far!*

I cry out, gritting my teeth at the burn of being stretched. He doesn't take his time or rub like I'm some cheap wind-up toy. I get the sense that he's merely testing me instead. Satisfied, he wrenches his fingers free.

I hiss through my teeth at the loss. My legs are quivering, my heartbeat unsteady. I can't seem to catch enough air as he raises his palm to his mouth and spits. When he moves that same hand to his cock, I know that he doesn't need the lubrication. He's doing it to prove a point—this is what he thinks of me. A whore he can take selfishly without preparation. A slut.

Someone desperate enough not to care either way.

Selfishly, he guides himself forward while snatching a fistful of my hair with his free hand. He tugs, slamming his hips forward in the same swift motion.

There is no resistance. At first. It's like my body has become so accustomed to average men that his balls are striking against my ass by the time I register just how deep he truly is. How massive.

My lips fly apart, my voice a squeak. "You're so big."

He grunts in annoyance, pinching my inner thigh—but I'm not lying.

He's verging on the edge of painful, every thrust like being rubbed raw from the inside out. But when he eases himself nearly all the way out, the friction is like dropping a lit match over a trail of gasoline.

A strangled cry echoes back to me, and it's a second before I realize that it's me. It's been so long since I've felt something so intense. Nerves I'd forgotten existed come alive, begging for attention.

From him.

And he somehow manages to stimulate every last one as he shoves himself back in, slamming home with a grunt.

Even his sounds feed the tempests of sensation washing over me, addling my senses. I rock my hips into his next thrust. Groan when he slides out. Again. Again.

We're jerking across the mattress. Soon, my head slips off entirely, dangling over the floor as he grips me tighter, increasing his pace.

It's so damn good.

I'm whimpering beneath the onslaught, feeling my belly tighten like a rubber band stretched taut. Too taut. Snap!

My spine arches, fingers grappling for a fistful of the sheets. Orgasm, I realize. I can't remember the last time I had one like this. So intense I can feel every muscle clamping down over his cock. Every pulsating ridge of muscle ramming inside me, heedless of the way my entire body tenses.

My lips are open, but I'm too breathless to make a sound, my eyes on the opposite wall as my head lolls in time to his movements, slamming off the mattress.

"Fuck!" He lunges, sinking his teeth against my collar bone.

I can feel him coming inside me, and it's seemingly endless. I'll burst from the force of it, but he's already wrenching himself free.

Don't let him go.

The thought drives me to muster my aching limbs into motion. I grab him, finding his mouth, kissing him with all I have.

Tire him.

I don't think. I crawl onto my knees, shoving him back.

As his eyes meet mine, I freeze, waiting for him to shove me off. His gaze narrows instead. Impatient.

Without needing a prompt, I rake my fingers down his chest, tug at the remaining buttons holding his shirt together.

"Don't." He bats my hands away, but inclines his head lower.

Somehow, his cock is semi-hard, practically lurching into my hands. I ignore my hesitation and lower my head, taking him into my mouth as deeply as I can.

"Shit!" His fingers grapple for my hair, grabbing chunks so hard my eyes water.

I suck him like a starving woman, ignoring the taste. Until I can't, forced to acknowledge that it's nowhere near as repulsive as it should be. We taste like salt and sin together. Wrong and right. So damn good it makes my heart ache.

"Enough." He's thickening again, swelling over my tongue, but I don't stop. I can't. The desperate need to keep him here dulls me to everything else. Like common sense warning me to heed him. Like fear.

When he tugs on my collar, ripping my head free, I choke out a reply as his eyes flash dangerously.

"I've always wanted to taste you." My voice is so breathless, he can't tell if I'm lying. Am I?

Confused, he watches me, but he doesn't shove me off.

I return to sucking him, surprised by the pulsating ache between my legs. I'm so sore, overly sensitive from an orgasm.

And yet, I could take him again. God, some sick part of me wants to. Needs to. I'm writhing, rubbing my thighs together just to dull the ache.

"Jesus Christ," he says throatily. I can't tell if it's my mouth he's referring to or my arousal, tinging the air. My entire body betrays me. I couldn't hide my pleasure if I tried.

"Get on your knees." He pushes me back again, so abruptly that liquid sprays from my mouth, my lips still parted in an o-shape.

A smug gleam alights his eyes, setting my entire body on edge.

"Do it." He snatches my hair to make me comply faster, forcing me to spin, putting my back to him.

He doesn't waste time taunting me. He runs his finger down my spine before stroking directly over his new target.

I wince, real fear breaking through the lust.

Men have fondled my ass before, begging me to let them take me there. I heard that whores like Alexi preferred it, eliminating any risk of pregnancy, but I never was a fan.

When Domino nears that area, he doesn't beg for permission. He breaches me without warning, utilizing the hard tip of a thumb.

I shudder. "D-Don't." My act slips. I'm afraid.

He doesn't care, driving himself deeper as my muscles fight to keep him out. It's such a different violation than the other. My body can't make that part of me as ready. The only solution is to let myself relax into him and force my muscles to allow him in.

And the pleasure here is different, slow-burning and cautious.

"You'd let me take you here if I wanted?" he asks, his voice so thick I can barely make out the individual words. He thrusts in a little harder, venturing a fraction deeper, and my cry is too sharp to smother. "Hell yes, you would."

And that pleases him. Excites him.

He shoves me onto my hands, gripping my ass, and my teeth clatter as I try not to resist, bracing myself for the pain.

He enters my pussy instead, taking effort to go deep and hard.

This orgasm is harder to find. I have to reach between my legs, stroking my clit, finding it swollen and dripping as he thrusts in again. Lightning flashes with every stroke. Finally, release.

I groan, burying my mouth against the sheets to smother the noise.

He shouts, scratching me brutally as if in punishment.

He wanted to fuck me. Hurt me.

He didn't want to enjoy it so damn much.

CHAPTER ELEVEN

I get my wish. He pulls out of me but doesn't go far, lying on his back within the tangled sheets. My lungs burn as I try to catch my breath while dragging my legs together, feeling his seed drip freely between them.

If my life weren't already in question, I'd book an appointment at a clinic tomorrow—despite the implanted birth control I had placed in my arm just a few months ago. It's advertised to be good for four years at least, but this night alone will put that to the test.

I'm never this reckless. Even Tristan never took me raw, and I don't think he's filled a condom with half as much as what I feel inside me now.

Sex, in my experience, is normally such a boring, casual thing.

Neither term can even begin to apply to what just happened with Domino. That was something far different and far more violating. It was destruction. Being dipped into hellfire.

My overall body throbs badly enough to have been burned. I'm moaning with every breath, shaking as the high wears off and reality sets in. My back is wet with more than just sweat. The stench of blood intrudes on his masculine flavor. It's too much to handle all at once.

I just want to sleep.

But I can't.

Lifting my head, I look at him, only to realize that he's watching me. His eyes gleam, mockingly alert. I haven't even begun to tire him.

"Your little stunt won't get you anything from me," he says bluntly.

Concealing my disappointment, I lick my lips and wince as my tongue strikes an open wound. He bit me. "I… I don't want anything from you."

"Bullshit." He props himself on his elbows, an eyebrow raised with open suspicion. "You're so used to seducing men; I'm surprised your cunt doesn't have a credit card swipe. Did you think you could convince me to take you home if you fucked me? Be a good boy?"

I hate how he makes me sound.

"Then I'm sure I fit your standards," I bite back, picturing Alexi. Only as the words leave my mouth do I remember that I wasn't meant to see those photos.

And I might have just given away my entire fragile plan right on the verge of putting it into action.

"You don't know a damn thing about what I want," he counters, lying back, his eyes on the ceiling. As the seconds pass, I dare to hope that he missed my slip-up. "But if you thought to play your little mind games, it's too late. You should have tried to fuck me that first night. I still hadn't decided, then..."

"Decided to what?" I ask, falling right into the verbal trap he sprung.

"Sell you."

I wait for him to laugh or taunt, or otherwise reveal the joke for what it is. A joke. When he doesn't, I'm not surprised. Deep down, I think I already knew that his plans for me were far more nefarious than keeping me hostage.

And yet, even as my horror builds, all I can do is ask him, "Why?"

"Why else?" he replies, his tone as level as ever. We could be discussing the temperature of the room for all the emotion his voice conveys. "You are a Pavalos. You know better than anyone that the world runs on money."

He's right—and how much might he stand to gain by selling me? I don't want to know.

Instead, I just pray he goes to sleep while I visually measure the distance between me and the vial. No longer is this a long shot attempt—it has to work. I'm so close. I only have to shift over an inch and reach beneath the mattress to grab it.

But then comes the logistics of getting the medicine into the syringe and injecting him without drawing his notice.

Worry about that as you go, a part of me warns. I've come too far to back down now.

"You aren't curious," he points out, reinforcing that he's still very much awake. Fully in control. "I'll admit, selling you might not have been my original plan—" I shiver as palpable anger stretches his voice taut. If this is him holding back, I shudder to imagine what his original plan may have been. "But then I asked myself, why disrupt what was already in place?"

I catch that low note in his voice. It's a taunt, daring me to question.

"What do you mean?"

"Your boyfriend," he says. "Tristan, was that his name? He's been planning it for a while, Ada-Maria. To lure you somewhere far beyond your Daddy's control. Arrange for a violent 'kidnapping.' Have you whisked away right under his nose and profit from selling you to an underground trafficking ring. It was a pretty solid plan when all is said and done. One I'm sure he didn't devise on his own. All of it calculated to catapult him as the chosen media darling to speak out against the rampant violence against women crusade your father championed. Bravo—" he claps. "Sadly for him, he didn't plan everything as meticulously."

"You killed him," I rasp, but some of my initial horror is tempered by the grim reality that I don't believe he was lying.

My God…

I think back to how eager Tristan was to meet me, despite having blown off previous dates for important meetings or dinners with his father's influential contacts. I suspected he was planning his own political run.

One of the main reasons my father sent me in his direction in the first place.

But this… It's a level of ruthless, cruel calculation that has frankly become the norm in Terra Rodea. Everyone sees anyone else as either a prize to be won or a rung to step over on the ascent to power. Tristan, my father, Alexi. They're all one and the same.

Ironically, the only person I ever suspected to be any different lies beside me now, the most cut-throat and cynical of them all.

"His plan didn't go accordingly," Domino says, in response to my last accusation. He sounds so unbothered by it all. So cold.

Any remaining heat on my skin cools, and I'm freezing—and yet this moment feels too fragile that I don't dare slip beneath the covers.

"I always thought you were different from him," I say, though I'm not sure why I choose now to make this confession. Though, there's no better time than the present, especially if I can't find a way to escape, my destiny leaves no other chance to say these words to him. In a sense, it's cathartic to get them out. "My father. I used to think that you were too kind to belong in his orbit."

"Kind," he echoes with obvious skepticism at that word choice. "Was that before or after I performed hits on his enemies? Before or after I threatened his rivals and paid off the many women he fucked outside of his marriage? You have a warped perspective on kindness, Ada-Maria—"

"You were different," I insist tiredly. On paper, his actions are just as horrific as Roy Pavalos', but I always sensed an intangible quality to him that set him apart from the others. My father surrounded himself with cutthroats, cowards, and despots. None of them would drag me from a highway in the middle of the night without demanding something in return. None of them would make sure my mother always had her secret prescriptions filled while my father was too busy playing politician to care that she was dying.

I'm ashamed to admit it, but even I haven't been there for her. I love her, but from a distance, admiring her gentle calm and the grace I never inherited. The reality is we're virtual strangers. By the time I turned fifteen, she was already a specter in my father's shadow, meekly agreeing to send me away to a school rather than go against him. And yet Domino deferred to her with perhaps even more reverence that he displayed toward my father. No one else blended duty with humanity the way he did. I saw it myself.

"So naïve," he murmurs.

Something disrupts my matted, sweat-soaked hair—his hand, I realize, running over my scalp to smooth back the strands.

"So trusting. You hit the trifecta, Ada-Maria. Saint fucking Teresa herself."

"You don't have to mock me." I shift away from him before I remember how important it is that I remain close to the edge, focused on my ultimate goal. I can't let emotion distract me now. I'm so close.

"You're right." He starts to sit up, twisting toward the opposite end of the mattress.

"Wait!" I reach for him, desperate to keep him here any way I can. "Just tell me why. Just tell me, please!"

He pauses, reaching out to graze my jawline with the pad of his thumb. "I like you desperate," he admits. "So eager to please. Keep this up, and you'll fetch me a hefty penny at auction."

I flinch. *Auction?* That term was designed to throw me off even more than he already has. It's working.

"I just want to know," I say, marveling at the fact that he hasn't shrugged me off. "Were you planning to betray my family all this time? Please…"

"You seem very interested in initiating pillow talk," he says softly. "I assumed your Tristan wanted to sell you for the clout and money it would garner him. I think I had it all wrong."

It's a low blow that resonates more deeply than I'll ever admit. My eyes sting with the threat of tears. Suppressing them is my first impulse, but I can't. They fall freely, and Domino's eyes narrow.

He drags his thumb up to capture one, watching it break open against his skin.

"Fine," I say, pulling away to curl onto my side. I'm taking a risk by doing so. But it seems to be the only way to reach him. To provoke him outright. "Leave. Prove me wrong. You're just like him."

I don't turn to see how my words land. If anything, I almost hope he does leave. A million different realizations are waiting to descend the second he's gone. I'll have to face the aftermath of everything he's revealed and everything I've done…

For now, he stays.

"I want to hear you say it," he proposes, still in that unsettlingly deep tone. "You say you wanted me. Why? What gets little Ada-Maria's pussy so damn wet?"

I cringe at the crass language. My only rebuttal is that same childish statement. "You were different."

He's sexy enough, but deep down, I can admit to myself that his personality was what kept me watching—the mystery of who Domino Valenciaga might be at his core.

Someone different, I'd hoped, far from the norm of bastards I grew up around.

And yet, he's not satisfied. "How?" His fingers creep through my hair again, this time tugging as he goes, irritating my already sore scalp. "What about me was so damn special to you?"

"You could ignore me," I croak, hating how pathetic my voice sounds in comparison to his. Weak. Vulnerable. He doesn't scoff or deny me outright. No one could lie so tragically. "You didn't treat me like some trophy. You watched everything and everyone. You seemed fair."

Men in far lower positions of power than him lorded their influence greedily. As Roy Pavalos' righthand man, he could have commanded an entire slew of lackeys and women in his own right.

Though, apparently, he had.

I'm dying to ask him about Alexi. How long has he been fucking her, and why? It couldn't be for her thrilling intellect. It's aggravating how deeply the bitch managed to integrate herself into my life. First Pia. Now any man I take an interest in.

No one in my orbit is spared her insidious influence.

My assessment of him, however, only seems to amuse Domino. He laughs. "A fair man with an interest in being easily seduced—" a sharp reminder of my last slip-up. Thank God he can't see my face. "You watched me enough to categorize the women I fuck?"

There's another taunt lurking somewhere within that phrasing. More importantly, I sense a trap. *Damn.*

"I… I didn't have to," I say carefully. "I saw the closet. You must keep this place busy with a wardrobe as large as that—and expensive. I don't even think my wardrobe is as well stocked."

And considering that my only value to my father extended to how I dressed and how he could use my appearance to his advantage, that says a lot.

Domino continues to chuckle, and I stiffen at the sound. It's harsher. Angry? As if he didn't mean for me to see that part of this room.

"I'll make sure Ines is more careful when selecting your clothing from now on," he warns, and I shudder at the thought of getting the woman into trouble. Though, as he continues stroking my hair, I get the sense that the brunt of his irritation is directed toward me. "As for your little assumption, you're wrong. Four days ago, was the first time I ever set foot in this house. Not long enough to parade a stream of women through it, unfortunately."

I marvel at that. He supposedly came here the same day as my abduction, or close to it. Meaning he's been planning this for a while. Just how long? Perhaps since the day he was first hired…

"So you've killed my father. Then you sell me. And then what?" I ask, unsure if I even want to know the answer. "My father has enemies, but he has allies too. Men who will hunt you down like an animal."

"You forget that I know those men far better than you do," he points out. "I am always one step ahead, Ada-Maria. The police are still scanning the restaurant, hunting for clues of your disappearance."

I notice that he specifically doesn't mention my father. If he were really dead, all of Terra Rodea would be in an uproar, and any missing figure from my father's orbit would be a suspect. His face is probably plastered all over the city on notices stating he's wanted for questioning.

Which means wherever this place is, he's confident no one will find me here. At least not right away.

"We aren't near Terra Rodea," I say, risking taking my eyes from him long enough to glance from the window.

"No. We are far away from Terra. Far from the state. Far from the country."

And somehow, he managed all of this within hours, transporting me supposedly out of the country, all without catching the notice of the authorities.

"Why me?" I ask him, returning my gaze to his face. "I never did anything to you."

"You want to sleep, then sleep," he says. "The rumors were true—your mouth is much more bearable with a cock stuffed in it."

I cringe, my face heating. I hate the thought of him throwing those rumors in my face. Rumors I know for a fact were driven by Alexi.

But he's right. I want to sleep. I want *him* to sleep, and hopefully when he does…

I'll be ready to act.

I startle awake, blinking rapidly through the darkness. Within seconds I realize I'm still in that white room, though now it's bathed in shadow, the lights off. As I sense the mattress beneath me, my heart plummets with a mixture of dread and shame.

Damn it. I failed, letting down my guard long enough to drift off. Domino is gone, and I've blown my one shot at freedom. Numb with despair, I try to sit up and realize that my hair is tangled in something. In *someone*, their fingers, to be exact...

He hasn't left.

Slow and steady, his breath fills the air as a dangerous lullaby. I gather the nerve to look up, catching the chiseled line of his jaw, barely visible in the dark. He's actually asleep, and a terrifying question comes to mind. How long have we been like this?

Beyond the windows, the sky is pitch dark. Hope creeps up

my throat as I look back at Domino. I raise my hand, waving it through the air. He doesn't stir.

Slowly, I gather the nerve to roll unto my side next, lifting my head as high as I dare.

His hand falls free, but he doesn't move. His eyes are closed, his chest rising and falling steadily. He's asleep, and I nearly exhale in relief—only the fear that the sound might wake him keeps me silent.

What now?

My first thought is to scan the bed, searching for my dress, I find it slung over the end of the mattress, and I pull it on, ignoring my disgust at the stickiness coating my inner thighs. My lips…

Shaking my head, I try to focus. Carefully, I inch toward the end of the mattress, holding my breath as I feel along the seam between it and the bed frame. *No. No…*

Here! I clutch the smooth surface of the vial and wiggle it free. *Shit!* It slips from my grasp, rolling across the floor.

My heart falls along with it. There it is. I've blown my chance. I wait for Domino to wake up, but he doesn't move. I strain my ears to track the rhythm of his breathing. Slow and steady, still. He's asleep.

I don't waste any more effort on stealth. I lurch to my feet, racing on tiptoe for the vial. Then I grab the syringe, trying to remove the plastic casing without making too much noise. It's an eternity before I finally get it free and ease off the plastic cap covering the needle. It's so dark in this room. All I have are glimmers of a faint glow entering from the windows. Yard lights?

They barely illuminate the glass of the vial enough for me to find the rubbery top through which I can inject the needle.

Luckily, muscle memory takes over. Ironically, as far as drug use goes, my injecting phase didn't last long. It was too risky. Too ugly, leaving angry red marks that threatened my one defining attribute—beauty.

I switched to snorting and never looked back, but you never forget the intricacies of manipulating a syringe. Though, I don't think this needs a vein. Just muscle. Like an arm or a thigh.

Eyeing the bed, my gaze fixates on one of his outstretched legs, and I decide on my method.

For all my confidence, my hand shakes so badly that the needle goes into the vial crooked on my first attempt to fill the syringe. When I pull back on the plunger, liquid seeps through the rubber top, but I keep going. How much should I pull up? Is the whole vial too much?

I can't remember the dosage, so I just draw back until I can't anymore. The liquid glows amber in the faint orange light. It nearly fills the entire barrel, and for a second, I weigh the possibility that I could potentially give him an overdose. Kill him.

My finger jerks, spilling some of the liquid onto the floor, but there's still plenty left, and my conscience is a little lighter.

Though why the hell should I care at all? This man is a monster, and as I rise and pivot on my heel, I realize that if I do manage to hit a vein when I inject the needle, I could kill him with this. If not with the drug alone, then the infection he'll get from my sweaty, filthy hands, and the lack of sanitation.

But I don't have a choice.

Cautiously, I reach for his thigh, touching him as lightly as I can. Hard bone flexes beneath my fingertips. His knee? I go higher, until I find the thicker, sturdier feel of solid muscle.

Then I aim and stab, shoving the plunger down.

"What the fuck?" He comes alive swinging, easily snagging my hair in the dark—but not the chain.

I clutch the length of it in my palm and leverage my weight against him, ignoring the pain as strands of my hair are ripped clean from their roots.

"No!" I lunge for the door with everything I have.

Somehow, I break away, and I don't look back, staggering into the hall, racing for the circular room.

"You bitch!"

I can hear him raging behind me, crashing like a bull.

Don't look! I just move, despairing as I reach that round door, sure it will be locked. But when I throw my weight against it, it opens.

I race on bare feet down the stone path, meeting no one to stop me. It feels easy. Too easy, but the doubt isn't enough to make me second guess this plan.

I've come too damn far.

So I run, my lungs heaving, muscles aching. Still, I don't stop until the ground beneath my feet switches to dried, rough earth. It strikes me now that I have no idea of where to go or which direction civilization may be.

It's not like I have a choice to stop and plot.

All I can do is run.

CHAPTER THIRTEEN

I t isn't long before I realize that my "escape" is just an illusion.

This has always been a game from the start.

The sun rises, first as a faint glimmer of pink over the horizon, and then turns into a sweltering ball within hours, scorching my body from overhead. The illumination throws into stark contrast just how barren this landscape is. It's the middle of nowhere. In either direction, I only find cactus, dry earth, and scraggly brush.

I've gone far enough from the house that I can't even see it at least. Though, it's not much of a comfort when I compare being held captive there to dying of heat exhaustion.

Or exhaustion in general—my entire body is a throbbing mass of pain. The golden chain, wrapped around my wrist, is a boiling hot iron shackle weighing me down, but I can't stop moving. The second I do, I doubt I'll have the strength to get up again. Sheer desperation is the only thing keeping me going, even as the despair gets harder and harder to ignore.

No wonder he kept the doors unlocked, and the staff never stopped me from leaving. There's nowhere to go.

This place must be miles from any town or even a gas station.

And I don't have the strength to make it that far. My steps are sluggish and staggering as the heat drives out what little liquid remains in my body as sweat.

When I first see the approaching car in the distance, I'm stupid enough to feel a tendril of hope. I even turn to it, limping, my throat so dry it hurts to suck in the air needed to speak, let alone scream. *Help me…*

Then common sense descends once I note the speed of said vehicle—a pace vicious enough to kick up billows of swirling dust that engulf it like a storm cloud. *Run!*

I try, painfully aware of the roar of an engine easily eating up the distance between us. Every grueling, punishing step feels like it lasts an eternity, but it must be mere seconds before the car advances on my position, roaring like an animal. Veering around me, kicking up dirt and dust, it skids to a stop paces away. I've barely remarked that it's too expensive to belong to the average desert joyrider—some imported luxury sort, I bet—when the driver's side door flies open, and Domino climbs out.

Shock alone knocks me off balance. I fall on my side, crying out. My carefully wound chain comes undone, biting into the earth as a jagged mass.

One look at him, and I know my plan failed. He's standing upright, moving easily. Considering that same drug supposedly knocked me out for hours, I doubt a whole syringe wouldn't have any effect on him.

"Did you really think that would work, Ada-Maria?" he demands. Anger rips through each syllable, matching the ire flashing in his eyes. "That you could drug me and just prance away? That I would really make it that easy for you? Do you want to know what you really injected me with, Ada? The equivalent of vitamins."

I can't tell if he's lying or not. But nothing else could explain why he's here now, on his feet, obviously alert.

"I even had Ines prepare a wonderful breakfast in case you decided to come crawling back on your own," he adds, presumably his reasoning for why it took him so long to come after me. He wasn't drugged. He was gloating. "Shame you missed it. Though you can still run if you want." He forms a visor with his hand and comically scans the horizon. "Go ahead. Spend the day running to freedom. You wouldn't even get close. There is no one to save you here."

It's as if his words are the trigger for every ounce of pain, weakness, and exhaustion I've kept at bay until now. I break.

My sobs are dry and gasping with no real tears to show for them. Just teasing hints of moisture that blurs my vision and stings my eyes even more in the brutal sun.

"You're here until I tire with you," I hear him say over me. "After last night, that moment is drawing nearer, Ada. Look up."

He snaps his fingers, commanding me to.

But I can't. *So close...* My eyes downcast, I clench fistfuls of the brown dust beneath me and watch it filter away on a gust of wind.

I was so close.

The thought haunts me, regardless of if it were true or not. As long as I kept moving, I felt close. Brave. Strong. All of those things I never was.

Without my father, I was always nothing. Am nothing.

It was a mindset my mother instilled, abiding by that very creed until she was wasting away before him, and he didn't even notice. She let Roy Pavalos consume her and groomed me to sacrifice myself in the same way.

But I *can't...*

"Come here." I see his shadow as he lunges for me, but I don't move. Not even as he snatches the chain from the ground, unwinding the tangled mass. "You were quite convincing; I'll give you that," he says, letting the chain loosen as he returns to the car. "Spinning your little lies. Trying to get my guard down. Using the one talent you do have. I'll be sure to add that skillful mouth of yours to the listing. Those bastards at *La Guarida del Tigre* will have fun with that."

La Guarida…

I lose track of the thought as he braces his free hand against the car's sideview mirror and wraps his length of the chain around it.

"Think about how many other talents you might have to save yourself, Ada-Maria. Because when I get you back to the house…"

He lets the threat hang in the stifling air, conveying the same promise as a death sentence. I can't run anymore. I can't fight him. All I have to combat him with are three pathetic words.

"I hate you."

He scoffs and tugs on the chain, yanking me forward. I barely manage to brace my hands over the dirt to catch myself.

"Move."

He climbs into the car, slamming the door after him. I consider lying here, unmoving, letting the heat and exhaustion finish me off. I barely have the energy to stand. Slowly, I attempt to, groaning as I rise to my knees.

And the car begins to move.

As does his end of the chain. Unraveling, the coils of gold kick up dust as it extends with every inch of distance he gains, until…

Clink!

It's like being caught on a fishing line. I have no choice but to crawl in the direction of the pulling force. Stagger. Fall. Stand. Run.

Die.

He doesn't relent, no matter how many times I trip. The chain gets so tight I swear it will snap. Frantic, I grip it with both hands in a vain attempt to loosen the pressure. Then it becomes my only stabilizing force to find my balance.

The sun bears down, blindingly hot, until I can't see the car. I can't see anything. What a fitting metaphor for the hell my life has become—well before the kidnapping. Two years ago, I finally tried to take steps to end it.

And I failed.

If anything, this moment is the chance to finally make up for that regret.

So, I close my eyes as the chain grows tighter, cinching my throat.

And I just let go.

"ADA! YOU LOOK AT ME! ADA!"

I can't breathe. It's just a relief. At the same time, it hurts. My lungs are on fire, my throat crushed. Even as I try to suck in air, I can't.

I'm dying.

"Shit—"

A metal clang sounds. Then air…

I suck in with faint, stingy breaths, but it's enough that my lungs fill. Too late do I realize that I've blown yet another chance.

Because of the same man who foiled my prior attempt.

"You look at me," he demands, his voice like sin, his eyes blazing like fire. "You look at me."

He's scowling, though his voice lacks any anger or rage. He just sounds bitter. A man too devoid of emotion to feel anything in this moment but aggravation.

He stands, but I feel myself being lifted as well. Into his arms, I realize. My vision blinks in and out of focus.

When I come to again, I'm shrouded from the sun, someplace darker. In a car? The engine roars beneath me as my head lulls with the force of the motion.

The driver's back is to me, but his scent is life-giving, sustaining my body when every inch feels broken and battered.

"I…" Trying to speak is excruciating.

He doesn't react, but it feels suddenly important to say it, if only for myself.

"I've loved you…since that day. On the road. I did. But you were just like them…"

And he just happened to join the long list of people I ever cared about.

My mother.

My father.

Pia.

Alexi…

In their own way, they all sold me, in the end. He just went about the most literal method of doing so.

CHAPTER FOURTEEN

The world is wonderfully quiet. And warm. And peaceful. And perfect.

Until noise crashes through my beautiful, white wonderland of unconsciousness. It's faint, as if heard from a radio, but I can't deny a sign of the real world rudely intruding upon my private sliver of heaven.

"…beginning to think you're reneging on our agreement, Dom."

"I told you," a man replies, his voice cold. "I got carried away. It's only been a week. She needs another one here at least. Unless you want her price cut to a third of what you could get for her. That's if she doesn't scar."

"If I didn't know better, I'd assume you played roughly with your toy on purpose," the first speaker scolds. "That way, you don't have to share. But you wouldn't be so sloppy as to do that, would you, Dom? She was your bargaining chip to bring me in. You change your terms, then I'm entitled to change mine. Take your week. Though, I might pay you a visit to ensure there are no more mishaps. You can play with your toy, but don't forget that technically, little brother, she belongs to me."

"You're more than welcome to take her from me. That is, if you have the balls, *big brother*."

"At least I *do* still have mine," the man counters. "Ada Pavalos already has yours in her manicured little hands, doesn't she? A week, Dom. No more."

Silence falls again, but it feels fragile, broken more frequently by various soft noises as if a veil is slowly being lifted…

Until everything is free to assault me all at once. Chirping insects. Muffling footsteps. More noise, noise, noise…

And a voice.

"Hold off on reinserting the tube," a man says, his tone resonating authority. "Her last dose should be wearing off. I'll see if she'll eat by mouth. Keep the equipment near, just in case."

Whoever he's referring to, he must hate. Utterly loath. Thinking of the negative emotions makes my head ache. Pain is cruel, creeping into my delicate realm of peace. My head. My skin. Everything, *everywhere*.

I just want to sleep, but with every passing second, I feel that oblivion slipping further and further away. Soon, the white haze around me turns brighter, pierced with bits of yellow. Sunlight. It's so vivid, like droplets of gold, shining so bright it hurts. I try squeezing my eyes shut and wind up blinking.

Gradually, my protective cocoon shatters, revealing the reality lurking beneath. I'm in a room, one decorated in shades of white and tan and a mockingly blue sky viewed beyond a row of windows. I think it's meant to be as beautiful and relaxing as my hazy dreamland.

But it isn't. My heart is already racing, my nerves prickling with an awareness that all isn't as it seems. This room is dangerous. So is this place…along with the scent seeping through my lungs with every frantic breath I take.

It's so spicy it burns with every exhale, conjuring memories that flicker at the back of my exhausted brain. A man. A terrifying man.

Domino.

His face fills my vision at the exact moment that name flashes across my consciousness. A sun-kissed gold, his skin gleams, his eyes shrouded by thick lashes, the rigid planes of his face set in a stern mask.

"You're awake," he says with no inflection. "Ines will be around in an hour with your meal. I suggest you eat it."

He stands, revealing that he was seated in a leather chair placed beside the bed. All black, it's glaringly out of place, as is the starkly metal structure looming behind him. It's something medical, I think. My head is throbbing too badly to properly identify it.

God, I just want to sleep.

I can barely process the words being spoken to me next. "…suggest you don't try to get up. Later, someone will come to change your bandages."

My brain sluggishly processes each syllable. *Bandages?*

That word spurs me to look down. Alarmed, I find that my body doesn't exist anymore. All I discover is just a seamless space of white where it should be. Until I move, and the whiteness moves with me. Blankets. Slowly, I strip them away. Beneath, my limbs are whiter than the fabric, damn-near blue, and pink and brown. I'm a patchwork of colors and textures. Tiny spots of dark purplish flesh. Jagged lines of scarlet. Splotches of raw, scabbed skin.

Then strips of white. Bandages. Like I've been ripped to pieces and put back together with glue. A Frankenstein monster of wounds and injuries.

The panic I feel is like a living thing, ripping through my insides, distracting from any other thought. I'm hideous, my one defining attribute gone.

Because he didn't kill me.

I look up and realize he's left the room. The harsher details I didn't notice before stand out. One of the windows is open, allowing in the warm air scented with flowers. I'm back at the mansion, even though I remember running. Confused, I scramble to view my feet and cry out in a mixture of pain and alarm.

They're both wrapped in bandages, but I can feel the raw skin beneath. Blisters and torn flesh ripped away by the dirt.

I walked on foot for only God knows how long.

And I was dragged back.

A hopelessness unlike any I've ever felt sucks my breath away. It's chilling and all-consuming. I just sink inside myself, knowing there is no way out.

No hope.

But I tried. I remember stabbing him with the medicine, and injecting him with some of it. From what I vaguely remember, he didn't seem drugged in the slightest when he approached me in the desert.

Did you really think that would work, Ada-Maria?

Somehow, he knew…

"Your meal, Miss."

I look up to find Ines at the doorway, a silver tray in hand. She advances toward the bed and places it on the rumpled sheets beside me. On it is a bowl of red liquid smelling faintly of tomatoes, a small dish of red berries in a gelatin mixture, and a piece of toast.

The color scheme of the meal seems deliberately designed to resemble my body's current state—burned and bloodied.

I'm not hungry. I try to voice my refusal, but my throat…

It's in agony, so sore even thinking of trying to speak triggers a sharp pain. Gingerly, I trace my fingers along it. The skin feels tender to the touch, scraped raw—but the collar is gone, I realize with a start.

So is the chain.

"Mr. Domino would like you to eat, Miss," Ines says, her soft voice conveying a clear warning.

Domino *commands*.

A wave of white-hot anger washes over me. I only register grabbing the edge of the tray, but it's like I'm watching a stranger throw it across the room. Or attempt to. It's too heavy for me to fully lift, and the tray and its contents merely land at the foot of the bed, spilling across the floor like blood.

If Ines reacts, I don't stay to watch. Instead, I crawl to the end of the mattress and attempt to stand. My legs are wooden, slow to respond to my brain's commands. I have to physically shove them over the edge of the bed. My bandaged feet drag across the floor, and I know standing isn't in the realm of possibility.

So I slide from the bed instead, landing on my knees. My hands smart as I brace them flat and try to crawl in the direction of the mirror. I nearly give up, but vanity gives me the strength where all else fails. I need to see myself. Driven by that goal, I drag myself inch by inch, my cracked nails scraping the marble surface.

By the time I've cleared the side of the bed, I've come far enough to watch myself advancing in the mirror's surface. I'm a broken creature. A desiccated demon, crawling out of hell. My hair hangs limp and lifeless down my shoulders. All I'm wearing is a plain black bra and underwear—neither looks like a brand I personally own, but that's the least of my worries.

My arms and legs are riddled with bandages, but what's been left exposed isn't entirely unmarred skin. I'm a monster. A woeful creation of scratches, bruises, and skeletal limbs.

I'm disgusting, every bit as repulsive as the man I see entering the room claims I am to him.

I expect rage as his dark eyes take in the mess on the floor. Ines stands behind him, her hands neatly folded, head bowed respectfully.

Finally, his gaze settles over me, and I stiffen, waiting for the impending assault I know is coming.

"Ada-Maria will take her lunch on the terrace instead," he says. "Have cook prepare a serving for me, as well. I would like her room cleaned in the meantime. Unless..." His eyes narrow. "She would prefer to continue receiving her meals via a feeding tube?"

Feeding tube. For some reason, his tone draws my notice to the tall, skinny medical device behind him. It looks like an IV pole, with a square box affixed to a long, metal rod with hooks at one end meant to hang bags of fluid from.

Or liquid nutrition.

I've been threatened with a feeding tube once before, five years ago when I had no choice but to see my first therapist —an overzealous woman my father quickly replaced when she took my "depressive state" too seriously. The next one only prescribed pills and smiles, a perfect remedy for the daughter of a man perpetually in the spotlight. Baggy sweaters and loose dresses were enough to disguise my "unusually thin" frame before I learned which number on the scale could garner the least amount of attention without making me look like a whale. It became a game of sorts, threading the needle of that delicate BMI range.

How far could I endure the hunger before it threatened to consume me? As it turns out, for a long damn time. It's sick to pride myself on something so self-destructive, I know that. But knowing that didn't make it any easier to loosen the reigns of control I'd mastered so obsessively.

But I will never forget the sight of one of those machines meant to scare me into eating "normally."

I cradle my throat in both hands, horrified by the thought of a tube being shoved down it, my body pumped full of only God knows what.

"I think you should help Ada-Maria get dressed and meet me on the veranda, Ines," Domino says, turning for the doorway. "Since she seems so inclined to stretch her legs. I'll inform cook as to the change in plans myself."

"Yes, sir."

I stare after him, too terrified to resist Ines' gentle touch as she eases me onto my feet. I lean on her so heavily I'm sure she'll topple over, but she's surprisingly strong, able to haul me back to the bed before entering the closet.

A moment later, she returns, holding a white sundress by its delicate straps. When she helps me into it, it's loose enough to avoid aggravating my injuries. Though, as I take stock of myself in the mirror, I think the fact that I'm able to move at all is due to being drugged again. It's wearing off, enough so that I'm conscious, but the pain is a mere echo of what it must be. Excruciating. In addition to the injuries, my skin is sunburned, my nose peeling, my eyes bloodshot and dry.

How long was I out there before he came for me?

The thought makes me shudder.

"This way, Miss." Ines, once again, is forced to bear most of my weight as she guides me into the hall. It must be late in the evening, just before that golden hour of sunset. It's stifling, with nearly every window we pass open to let in what little breeze exists.

The circular room is empty this time, but just beyond the archway leading to the terrace is a set of white loungers, centered around a low table stocked with platters of fresh fruit, cheese, and crackers.

Domino commands one, a glass of red liquid in hand. He meets my gaze as he takes a sip. Then he nods to the space across from him. "Sit."

I deliberate running. The fact that I'm entirely dependent on Ines to stand is the only reason why I comply with his suggestion—she hauls me there herself, lowering me as he directed.

The chaise is luxuriously comfortable, and this area is shaded by several massive palm trees in terra cotta pots. As a result, the wrath of the sun is diminished to a gentle warmth, and, again, I get that eerie sense of being in most people's version of an ideal vacation home.

Minus Domino Valenciaga.

I try not to look at him at first, but as his lounger creaks with movement, I glance over to find him hunched over the table, piling various items onto a small plate. Finished, he hands it to me.

"Eat." A low rumble, his voice alludes to an unspoken warning. *So, help me God.*

A shiver runs down my spine. Even so, I consider throwing the plate over the balcony.

But then he'd drag me into that room and shove the tube into me himself. He will. That much is all but promised in his gaze. In fact, I think he prefers I disobey him.

So, I grab the plate and snatch an item at random. A grape that looms large as I raise it to my lips with trembling fingers. My throat feels so raw that eating anything at all feels more unappealing than ever. Still, I ease the grape into my mouth and bite.

I chew and chew, cringing at the sharp flavor. When I finally choke it down, tears spring to my eyes. I'd scream if I could; it hurts so damn much.

Still, I embrace the pain a second time to croak, "You disgust me."

He sits back, a lazy grin playing over his mouth as he balances his own plate on one palm. "Try the berries," he suggests dryly. "They're ripe and sweet."

It's a taunt. I can almost see the invisible threat he wields behind the request. I find one of the aforementioned berries on my plate and grip it between two fingers. Sweat beads over the back of my neck as I attempt to bring it to my mouth.

Then I choke it down, squirming at the thought of it sliding down my throat, filling my stomach.

He's watching me, I realize. Sharp with avid interest, he tracks my every move.

"Why didn't you just let me die?" I ask. It's a thought that haunts me as I recall just how close I must have been to that reality. Another hour in the sun. A few more feet of being dragged behind his car…

It's as if the universe is conspiring to bring me just to the brink, over and over again.

"You're worth more to me alive," he says.

"Because you want to sell me," I rasp. "Was that always your plan? Is that why you saved me before? To bide your time for five years?"

He chuckles. "*You saved me. You saved me.* Your imagination gets away from you, Ada-Maria. So prone to exaggeration—"

"I was lying on the highway," I say. Did he really have such a low opinion of me? To think that all I wanted was attention.

But I didn't.

And, naively, I assumed he knew that. That he cared.

His expression hardens again, unreadable.

"Why not now?" I demand, setting the plate aside as the remnants of the berry churn in my stomach. "Sell me now."

He raises a single dark eyebrow. "You're that eager to be paraded on auction before a bunch of bastards willing to buy you? They won't intend to take you out to some fancy restaurant, Ada-Maria, I can assure you of that."

I cringe, but I see through the taunt to his real motive. He *wants* me afraid. He thinks the prospect of that scares me. It does.

But one factor outweighs any potential horror that might await me.

"I'd prefer anyone to you."

"No, you wouldn't." He sits forward, his jaw tense. "I can promise you that."

I try to ignore how earnestly he says that.

"I hate you." I've told him that before, I think. Shouted it.

He cocks his head, dropping his plate onto the edge of the table as if he means to lunge across it. "Good. Your hate means nothing outside of the walls of that fancy house of yours, Ada-Maria. Without your Papa here to wipe your ass and pay your bills, your only worth to anyone is as a body. A warm, wet hole. You'll learn soon enough."

He sounds so serious. As if he doesn't truly realize that he just described the only worth I've ever had from the very start.

I close my eyes, swaying as the air sticks in my lungs and my breathing feathers.

"I want you to sell me," I say hoarsely. God, it scares me how honest I sound. Genuinely ready. "Sell me now. Anyone and anything will be better than you."

And now I can say that truthfully, I realize in horror. I'm armed with the experience of what it's like to have him firsthand. I cringe from the memories, craving anything harsher to replace them. Old men with breath like stale cigars. Greedy lawyers with small dicks and no lasting power.

All of them never pretended to be more. I never expected more. Never wanted more.

"Do it," I hear myself beg in a whisper. "Just sell me. Get me far away from you—"

"You don't want that." His voice is deeper, radiating a warning. *Tread carefully.*

I open my eyes to find him standing before me, grasping my chin with one hand. He's careful this time, applying just enough pressure to force my head back, leaving me no choice but to meet his gaze.

"We can play this your way," he tells me, stroking along my jaw with his free hand. "I'll coddle you, Ada-Maria. I'll hold your hand and treat you like a goddamn princess. Then you give me what I want—" He leans in, brushing his lips against my earlobe. "And then, you can gladly take the hundreds of cocks awaiting you after me, and you can comfort yourself with the fact that I gave you the one thing they won't. It's mercy."

Mercy. My mouth is still wet from the berries, so when I spit, it comes out red like blood, splattering his forearm.

He eyes the liquid with a sigh, an eyebrow raised. I tense, waiting for him to strike me. He smooths a piece of hair behind my ear instead. Gently.

"When you heal enough, I'll make you wish you didn't do that, Ada-Maria," he says. "Count yourself lucky that I am a forgiving man."

He releases me, reclaiming his lounger.

"Forgiving? You are a monster."

He tilts his head as if he never heard the term applied to himself before. Then he nods and grabs a grape from the platter, popping it into his mouth. "I don't think you're in a position to judge the moral character of anyone."

The words sting. They're meant to, designed to keep me on the defense, reacting out of anger. And stop me from asking him the questions he doesn't want to answer.

"When are you going to sell me?" I ask.

He shrugs. "When I grow bored of you."

He's lying. A snippet of conversation returns to me, muddled like static and hard to parse through. *A week,* I remember someone saying.

"A week," I parrot out loud.

A hint of alarm flashes across his gaze, confirming the timeframe as correct.

But in his orbit, seven days might as well be seven years.

"Sell me now."

"Then tell me what I want to know," he counters, sitting forward. I've irritated him, but I don't think my talking is the sole cause.

"Sell me now," I repeat, watching him carefully. "Tonight… I'd take a thousand different cocks just to forget yours—"

There. He's more than angry; he's furious, looming larger, his muscles straining against the fabric of his shirt.

All because I dared to compare him to someone else.

"You'll get your wish soon enough," he growls. "And for the first few, I'll watch. I'll watch them brutalize you in ways you could never dream. This? You'll look back fondly on these days as heaven on earth."

He's not lying this time, which confuses me even more.

My eyes burn, they're so dry, but somehow tears manage to form regardless, sliding down my cheeks. "I don't think so, Domino. No matter how horrible they are, I will gladly forget you."

He's on his feet, and I'm sure he'll strike me this time. He lashes out, instead grabbing my plate.

"Eat—" He snatches an item seemingly at random and shoves it against my mouth.

Instinctively, I clamp my lips shut, turning away.

He hooks his fingers beneath my jaw, wrenching my head back around. Brutally, he continues to shove a piece of fruit against my lips so hard the flesh clips over my teeth.

I cry out, and he lets go, dropping the plate onto the stones.

"D-Don't!" I nearly fall off the chaise in my rush to get away from him. I'll jump off this balcony if I have to.

As if reading my mind, he raises a hand. "Ada—"

"Sir." Ines' monotone voice is like ice water dumped onto a raging fire. We both whirl around to find her standing in the archway of the house, a cell phone in her outstretched hand. "Mr. Jaguar is on the phone for you."

Domino blinks, raking a hand through his hair. "Tell him I'll call him back—"

"He says it's urgent," Ines replies. "Regarding your business back in Terra Rodea."

Domino's eyes widen. "I'll be there in a minute." He turns away, eyeing the mess of fruit scattered across the terrace. "Fuck! Can I get someone out here to clean up this mess?"

"Right away, sir," Ines replies. She rushes to gather up the spilled food herself as Domino storms inside. A second later, I catch his voice, uttered in a low tone, rapidly fading as if he's moving deeper into the house.

"You call me twice in one day? I'm not your fucking whipping boy."

The phone must be on speaker because I hear someone reply, though barely audible, their voice even gruffer than his. "Try ignoring my call again, and we'll test that theory, Dom. I may have let you keep your little toy, but that doesn't mean you get a vacation. I need you on the border. Tonight. A shipment is coming in, and I don't trust Vodello not to fuck us…"

"I will show you back to your room now, Miss." Ines stands before me, her hand outstretched, her expression as blank as ever. She's already cleaned up the food, piling everything neatly onto the platter.

I let her guide me back inside as my mind races. That man sounded familiar, the same figure he spoke to earlier. *Jaguar*, Ines said. A name? Or an alias?

It doesn't matter. What does is, for the first time since I've met him, I think I know a way inside Domino Valenciaga's brain. It turns out that he has the same weakness as any man—pride. A smart woman would be able to play on that. Play *him*.

But to be sure…

I startle to awareness as I'm lowered onto the mattress. We're already in my room, and Ines is swiftly retreating toward the hallway.

"Wait!" I call after her. "He's leaving, isn't he? Ask if I have to stay in here. Please."

She blinks, and I feel that I've caught her off guard. She has to remember which part of her script she needs to recite next. "You should get some rest," she says, her expression carefully blank.

"Please! Just ask him! Ask if I can leave the room. Please…"

She nods and scurries off, while I wait, so anxious I'm holding my breath. When footsteps return, I'm expecting Ines, but Domino is the one who appears, his brow furrowed with open suspicion.

"You want to take your chances in the desert at night this time, Ada?" he wonders. "Don't be fooled by the sun. The temperatures can plummet after nightfall, and I won't come after you quickly, should you try to run."

I lick my lips, contemplating my reply. I've toyed with enough men in my life that it should be easy to manipulate him. In a sense, I already have.

And then I wound up being dragged behind a moving car by my throat.

He's too dangerous to play with. I'll have to tread carefully, treating his ego like a loaded gun. But if he truly wants my admiration, he'll enjoy having me beg.

"Please," I shamelessly croak. "I… I just want to take a bath and stretch my legs. I won't leave the house."

He's advancing toward me in an instant, stroking his thumb from my lips, down to my jawline. It takes everything in me not to recoil.

"I warned you once not to treat me like one of your desperate little fucks," he says. "I'll let you roam to your heart's content, Ada. When I return, I better not find so much as a pretty little hair out of place. If so? I'll have you *begging* me to sell you—and it won't be some coy attempt to rile my pride, either."

He lets me go, marching into the hall as my heart pounds furiously enough to drown him out. I'm not as clever as I thought. He saw through even my little game on the terrace. And yet…

Did he play along out of pure amusement?

Or because he couldn't help himself…

A door slams, presumably the entrance to the mansion. I know he's gone without having to check. The entire atmosphere of the house shifts, and I can breathe somewhat easier.

But not by much.

Time is a constant adversary, but if I work quickly enough, I could use each passing minute to my benefit—or accidentally doom myself more than I already have.

All in all, I have a week to seduce Domino. To what aim? To convince him to let me go? To sell me sooner?

Either act feels preferable to submitting to his form of mercy. I need answers, no matter where my fate takes me. Who is Jaguar? The man he plans to sell me to? And for what purpose exactly?

Though I can guess.

My mind is buzzing as I try to stand on my own and wind up crawling to the closet. Groaning, I manage to open the door on my own and blink to take in the array of clothing.

When viewed the second time, this closet is overflowing in comparison to his. There's at least a full year's worth, and I figure that's without having to wear a single item twice. Obviously, he was lying. Maybe he hasn't dwelled in this particular house long, but he could have had the clothing shipped from somewhere else where he kept a steady stream of women wined and dined.

Or held captive.

Though in five years, I can admit that he wouldn't have much time to "play" with those toys, though. He barely left my father's side, let alone the estate, for longer than a few hours at a time. Once, I tried asking him about his family, during the holidays, I think.

He just nodded respectfully and ignored the question entirely. And all that time, he seethed in silence, hating my father, and hating me.

I can't dwell on that now.

I need to seduce him—*no*. I cringe at that word choice. It's too simple to describe manipulating a man like Domino. I need to get inside his head, whether he likes it or not.

I need to provoke him.

Of all these outfits, however, two modes of attack become clear. Aim for sex appeal with one of the skimpier, black ensembles, or try to claim innocence wearing one of the frothy white dresses like the one I am now.

No. I shake my head, irritated with my own thought process. It's too simple. No. No…

In fact, I've already tried both methods, and both have failed. But I did get him to fuck me using another route entirely—blatant honesty. Desperation.

And if I were desperate to screw him again, I wouldn't waste time on pretty dresses or makeup—none of that fluff has ever swayed him before. I can't resort to the same bag of tricks that I would use to confront a man like Tristan, who rarely thinks without his cock.

Domino uses his brain.

And mine is too damn sore to think. I'm exhausted enough to lie here unmoving and sink into the sleep waiting to descend.

But I can't.

Determined, I brace my hands against the wall and use the support to stand. Slowly, I limp into the room and then the hall, finding my way into the bathroom alone.

The spacious room looks surprisingly welcoming without Domino to taunt me from the clawfoot tub.

"Would you like to take a bath, Miss?"

I jump and nearly trip as I turn to see Ines standing behind me, hovering near the doorway.

"Y-Yes," I say.

Nodding, she starts forward and performs the same routine Domino did, running the water and gathering various materials.

She runs the water pleasantly warm, however.

"Your bandages are due to be changed," she explains before unraveling the ones on my feet. I wince as she helps me into the tub, but whatever she placed in the water feels soothing against the raw flesh.

I smother a groan as I lean my head back against the rim of the tub and let her work.

She washes my hair, combing through the damp strands, and supplies me with a rag to run between my legs. I'm frowning by the time the water finally turns cold, and she approaches me with a stack of towels.

"I will get a nightgown for you to wear, Miss." She starts for the door, but something makes me reach out, spraying water all over the floor.

"Wait! I… I'll find one on my own."

With the bath comes a renewed sense of clarity. I can think again.

And I know exactly the kind of stunt Domino can't ignore. Ironically, it's the same plan I thought of for five years. One I fantasized about, but never had the balls to implement. I had no problem approaching men—but his rejection was one I didn't think I could stomach.

So I never followed through on creeping into his guesthouse, finding his closet, and lying in his bed wearing one of his shirts as a blatant invitation.

This time, there is no thrill. Just a heavy sense of dread as I pad down the hall wearing only a towel. Perhaps she senses my intentions, because Ines vanishes as I creep past my room, toward that door near the end of this otherwise deserted hall.

The door is closed, and for a heartbeat, I'm sure he locked it, thwarting my attempt outright. When I twist the knob, it opens easily, but I have to feel along the wall for a light switch.

The bed has been left neatly made, the closet door closed as well—but the duffle is gone from its hiding place, this time resting in plain sight on top of the cabinet containing the watches. I'm sure the photos are gone, but I find them in the same pocket where I left them.

Like a dare.

Compared to how many times my past self may have envisioned this moment over and over, I don't take the time to agonize over which shirt of his to wear. There aren't many to choose from. In the end, I grab a white button-up and exchange it for my towel. Still dripping wet, I start for the bed.

But something makes me pause before I leave the closet entirely. I grab those pictures, flipping through them until I find the ones of Alexi. He's wearing a watch in one of them, visible on his wrist. Gold face with a scarred leather band.

I look for it among the selection in the case, but can't find the exact one. I grab a similar model, with a darker band instead of brown. It's large on my wrist as I slip it on.

When I reach his bed, I lie on my stomach across the very edge and inspect the pictures again.

Now that I've experienced his cock for myself, no wonder Alexi is smiling so damn hard, her blue eyes sparkling with the everlasting devotion of a dumb, blond bimbo.

We were friends once. I used to think her dumb expressions were endearing, her promiscuity inspiring. She was blessed with a body of a porn star that she didn't have to starve herself to maintain, always the bubbly one of our friend group.

Once, it was just the three of us, her, me, and Pia.

And Domino knew them both. How?

Immortalized in these photos, her sly smile doesn't give me any clues. I always assumed Pia was the one who turned her against me, at least a month before she went missing. One day, we three were as close as sisters, united by a shared, crippling sense of "rich daddy syndrome." Though, in Pia's case, minus the "rich" aspect.

Then one day, Pia was gone, and Alexi was too busy fucking anything that moved to seem to care. Years later, she went away to college, and when she returned, I was the bell of the town, and she went well out of her way to ensure that I couldn't ignore her.

Tristan was just the latest in a long line of men connected to me that Alexi made it her mission to conquer. She never told me why she hated me. She doesn't talk to me at all.

Not that I've sought her out. Some childhood memories deserve to be dead and buried.

Even old friends whom my entire world once revolved around.

CHAPTER FIFTEEN

He's here. I swear, it's like I close my eyes for one second, and open them to Domino Valenciaga bathed in the pinkish glow of dawn, his back to me, his chest bare. A part of me stirs, curious despite myself.

I've seen his cock, but little else of his body overall. And there is so much more to see. His back is ripped, straining with solid muscle that flexes in the faint sunlight streaming in through the windows. He has on a pair of jeans that look covered in dirt. Groaning, he reaches for the waistband and then kicks them down. Plain white briefs are the only thing shielding the full brunt of his ass from view.

I hate that he can still seem so damn beautiful after everything he's done. But I should know better than anyone that beauty is only skin deep.

Seemingly oblivious to the fact I'm awake, he enters the closet and snatches a white tee shirt from a hanger, wrenching it on over his head, along with a clean pair of black slacks. He must prefer this looser-fitting, less casual clothing to the uniform he wore while working for my father.

I watch him, content to believe that he hasn't realized I'm awake.

Until his voice rings out, rough with exhaustion. "This is the part where you get the fuck out." He turns to face me, hands at his sides, eyes narrowed over the sight of me, slumped on my side, hair shielding most of my face.

As I slept, I managed to scatter the photos all over the floor. One, however, seems stuck to my cheek as if I fell asleep eyeing it. I have to peel it off, ashamed as I realize which one I'm holding.

A shot depicting his hand, squeezing Alexi's breast as she arches into him, her eyes partially rolled into her head, her tongue between her teeth.

Disgust makes me angry. Bitter. Hateful.

But I have enough sense not to give in to it now. I already made it this far.

"This is the part where you reward me for being good," I say, not bothering to hide the pain and tiredness in my voice. Judging from the daylight, I probably slept hours, but it might as well have been seconds for the amount of good it did my body. "And you give me something. Anything."

He frowns, his gaze skeptical. He leaves the closet and stoops to snatch one of the pictures from the floor.

"You enjoy looking at these?" he asks, brandishing the photo in question—Alexi's legs spread wide, his hand on her inner thigh. He must have held the camera, straining to get just the right angle.

I want to hiss and make a crude, nasty remark about the rumors involving Alexi and herpes. Rumors I just made up.

Instead, I say, "Didn't you want me to? You left them for me for a reason."

I'm not sure until I see one of his eyebrows shoot up in amusement. Or perhaps it's admiration.

"You aren't as stupid as you pretend to be," he says, tossing the picture aside. "Ask your question."

He keeps coming toward the bed, and I lose track of what I should be focused on. Getting beneath his skin, trying to discover what he knows. Instead, I just gape at his body through my lashes and let the petty, jealous thoughts run wild.

Alexi had him first, and I have to wonder if he was any different with her than he was with me. Though, of course, he was—he wanted her, he merely humored me, knowing all along that I was plotting behind his back.

When it came to Alexi, he acted on his lust.

"How long have you been fucking her?" I ask, my throat still excruciatingly tender.

He frowns, running his hand along the dark stubble speckling his jaw. I doubt he's slept since he left. His yawn isn't for show, and I notice that his eyes are bloodshot as he continues to advance.

He snatches the picture I'm holding, eyeing it once before tossing it aside.

"Does it matter?" he demands.

It doesn't. Still, I can't resist prying. "She was fucking my boyfriend—all of them, actually. I'm not surprised she tried to climb you next. I'm more shocked that you let her."

He scoffs. "The high and mighty Ada-Maria Pavalos is sneering down her nose at me. How will I ever sleep?" He moves to the head of the bed and flicks the sheets back. "I thought I told you to get the fuck out—"

"We were friends once," I blurt, my gaze still glued to the image he threw. It landed upright within my reach, mocking me with its carefree, explicit depiction of raw lust and fun. Alexi's smiling in this one. The sex must have been good. I bet he teased her playfully and took her cowgirl style to watch her tits bounce.

He didn't pin her down like a conquest and grip the collar he had placed around her throat for leverage.

"I know," he says, surprising me. I look over to find him still standing, his gaze shrouded by a wayward lock of dark hair. "She told me all about you."

I stiffen, hating the implications of that. I may not have spoken to Alexi more than a fake greeting every now and again at some random social event throughout the past five years—but I know she hates me.

"All lies, I'm sure."

"Not lies," he counters, sounding surer of that than I like. "She told me all the things I could figure out for myself."

I look back at the floor as he moves. A heartbeat later, the mattress dips, presumably beneath his body weight.

"She told me that I didn't have a shot in hell with someone like you. That you would never know I existed if I didn't have a dollar sign beside my name."

That sounds like Alexi, the bitch.

"I'm surprised she wanted you, then," I snipe. "Especially if she thought I didn't."

The mattress moves again and his heat kissing my skin is the only warning I receive before my hair is drawn back from my face, gathered loosely in a fist.

"You want to know what I want?" He tugs, wrenching my head back until I'm forced to face him staring down from above. "I want you to get out of my bed."

A second ticks by, but he doesn't let go. Gradually, his gaze finds my mouth, narrowing further.

"You want to stay?" he asks. "Then prove it. Give me a reason to keep you."

His voice lowers in a way that makes me suspect exactly what he means, even before he snatches my wrist, dragging my hand toward him.

He doesn't stop until my fingers brush something warm, rigid, and firm bulging beneath the fabric of his slacks.

The right thing to do would be to run. Utter some coy quip about what else he can use to get himself off and save what little shreds of dignity I have left. I might do just that—if I had any pride at all. I'm too desperate for answers. Too desperate to feel like I'm doing something, even if it's playing a sick mind game at my own expense. I'll do whatever it takes to never feel as worthless as I did out in the desert.

"If I do it, what will you give me?" I ask him.

A new furrow appears in his brow—confusion. He didn't really believe I'd take him up on this offer. I can see him weighing the benefits of toying with me or maintaining the boundary between us. I can almost hear the question he must be proposing himself—*Can I really have my cake and eat it too?*

Or, in this case, abuse the mouth he loves to taunt. Before I know it, he has his thumb against the seam between my lips. He presses, ignoring how I wince as he aggravates the healing scrapes and marks left by his slap.

"If you do it... I'll give you exactly what you'd deserve," he says.

I shiver at the *double entendre*. Or maybe, in this case, there are a million different meanings, each one more biting than the last. *I deserve only his cum in my mouth. I deserve to suffer. I deserve to be sold. I deserve, I deserve...*

He pulls back as if expecting me to recoil now and do what he really wants—leave. He can't truly take the risk of letting me claw away another concession, another piece of him, no matter how small.

Alexi should have told him how selfish I am. How greedy, how stubborn. I'm the sort that even if I get hurt in the end, I'll still take the last cookie from the jar. No matter the overall cost, I'll still savor that brief taste of sugar. Or at least I would back when I still craved food at all. Hunger has been my constant companion long after my real friends vanished. It's the only thing I could trust, more satisfying than any cookie or piece of candy.

In this case, my "cookie" is more figurative. After years of craving him, a part of me can't resist experiencing what little I can, any way I can get it. At least then, I can square each session with that tiny bit of myself whispering that nothing is ever worth the effort. There's nothing worth fighting for. The world is shit; why not just starve until I fade away altogether.

That voice gets softer when I roll onto my aching side and press my cheek against his knee. One of his legs is outstretched, running parallel to me. The other he has braced against the floor.

Gradually, his expression shifts from wariness to a steely look I recognize. A dare. A demand.

My hands shake as I fumble with the latch of his slacks, folding down the fabric once I get it loose. That's about as much as I can do alone, I realize. He's too big to counter, and I don't have the strength to tug down his pants enough to have access to him.

Jaw clenched, he does it himself, working his cock free of his boxers. The state of him confirms my grim suspicion as to what aroused him to that extent before. It had to be my back. My blood.

This time, he only has my face to go off on, and he's barely firm, though still intimidating enough. It hurts to open my mouth wide enough to even consider taking him in. Then another consideration takes precedence—my throat is on fire, making the prospect of utilizing much beyond my tongue doubtful.

Not that he'll care. Still, I can't resist a desire to see his reaction if I dared to state as much out loud.

"My throat hurts," I rasp. "I don't think I can take you after all."

His eyes narrow, a smirk flitting across his mouth with breathtaking speed. One of his hands latches onto my skull, and there isn't even time to brace before he's guiding me lower.

The pain is worse than I could imagine. Burning and sharp as I stretch my jaw to accommodate him. I imagine healing bits of flesh being ripped open merely to satisfy his need for depth.

He groans the second he's enveloped in the heat of my mouth, my tongue cradling the underside. If I dull my senses and ignore the pain—and focus on the sheer act of taking him—there is a sick sense of pleasure a part of me gets out of feeling him stiffen. Harden. Swell.

He hates me, but he can't deny the simple pleasure even my battered mouth can provide. Soon, I feel his fingers flex, sinking into my hair, guiding my movements into a rhythm he likes. Slow. Steady. I can't tell if this is truly his preference, or if he's settling out of concern for me.

Then his nails scrape my skull as if to counter any chance of that second option. This is only about his pleasure, nothing more.

To prove it, he groans again, throatier than before, and I ignore the shame just to dissect the sounds he makes. Grunting boar is how I would describe most men—not him. He's nuanced, each groan or gasp conveying a different meaning.

Sharp and grated if I don't meet his expectations. Deep and rasping if I do. He praises me grudgingly with ragged, panting breaths that quicken as his grip on my head gets tighter and tighter.

I can almost track the ascent of his release through his shaft, but he surprises me by letting me go just as he nears that peak, allowing me to pull away if I wanted. And I should.

The first spurt catches me off guard, hot and molten. It feels like my throat is being boiled as I try to swallow. I can't. Coughing, I pull back, and his hand seizes another fistful of my hair to make me face him.

He continues to erupt, splattering the sheets and my chest. Satisfied, he shoves me away and turns to sit on the edge of the bed with his back to me.

"Alexi got one thing wrong," he admits gruffly. "She said you were shit in the sack. A doormat that lies there while it's being fucked." He parrots her voice, but he doesn't have to for me to know every word came from her.

I'm still swallowing him down, swiping my hand across my mouth. I'm shaking. Speaking is a daunting task, but it seems like he's waiting for me.

"Is…that…a compliment?"

He laughs. "No. It's an acknowledgment of your skill," he says, switching back to the mocking growl. "After all, you're the same girl who blew a banker to convince him to fund your father's fledgling campaign."

Ice. My entire body goes cold, and pain is an afterthought as I lurch upright.

"Where… Where did you hear that? Who told you that?"

He inclines his head, his eyes unfathomable again. "Who do you think?"

"Alexi couldn't," I rasp. She didn't know. No one did. No one but…

Domino levels me with a piercing glance. "*Who* do you think?"

"P-Pia?"

He doesn't answer. Standing, he adjusts his slacks and then nods to the doorway. "Get out."

I don't argue this time. I lurch to my feet and run—or, in this case, hobble. I don't stop until I'm back within that white room, crawling beneath the blankets.

Pia told him, he implied.

But how? Especially considering the fact that he seems convinced that she's dead.

Because he probably tracked her down, years later, and he killed her himself, at my father's behest.

CHAPTER SIXTEEN

I don't know how I fall asleep again—but a dream is the only reason to explain why I'm seeing her now.

Pia, her large upturned green eyes sparkling, a brown curl twisted around her finger. "Don't be so hard on yourself," she said. "If you bothered to wear something other than sweats, you'd have them eating out of the palm of your hand, too."

Them being the gaggle of older boys gathered on the tennis courts near the campus library. We were watching them from above, utilizing the last break before our final class of the day.

"Alexi's wearing sweats," I pointed out, nodding to her tight pink leggings and matching jacket, worn with the zipper pulled down to show her cleavage. Naturally. She wasn't wearing anything underneath it, or the pants for that matter.

"They've all already seen her naked, so she doesn't count,"

Pia remarked in that coy, cold way that could make her approval feel so damn valuable. Her shirt was worth a fraction of Alexi's entire outfit, and yet she wore it with a poise that made her the guiding star of our little trio. Alexi could have been naked right then, and most of the boys would have still snuck glances back at Pia, watching like a queen from our position atop the bleachers. "Alexi doesn't have what you do, and what you have is what men drool over."

"What's that?" I asked, still eyeing Alexi, who was in the middle of popping the round head of a red lollipop into her mouth.

"Innocence," Pia replied. "You have that look about you. That obsession factor. You're the kind of girl a man could spend his entire life chasing after. Alexi can have them panting after her now, but it's just a phase. It won't last. In ten years, she'll be lonely, still showing off her cleavage to get a date. But you? I bet you'll be married to the love of your life by then, happily ever after."

Pia was never wrong. At least while she was alive. It was part of her allure, that uncanny ability to seemingly know everything and everyone. Somehow, she even knew Domino.

What was his relationship with her like? Were they friends? Lovers? Who knew when it came to Pia…

There were so many things about her I'm still in the dark about. Her mystery was part of her charm. And her downfall.

"Mr. Domino requests you join him for lunch."

The soft voice intrudes on the memory, and it scatters. I open my eyes to the quiet darkness found beneath the blankets. When I lift them aside, I find Ines standing at the foot of my bed, displaying a sleek black dress on its hanger.

"Ten minutes," she warns, laying the dress over the foot of the bed. "I will assist—"

"I want to get dressed on my own," I stammer. "Please," I add, as Ines blinks, startled by the request.

She flits her gaze nervously toward the door. "I am not sure…"

"Ten minutes," I say, lurching to my feet. "I'll be there."

Finally, she nods and retreats, more than likely to find Domino and alert him of my insolence.

Which means I need to make this stunt even better than the last. This plan feels like crawling ten steps forward, only to be shoved back past the starting line—but I did get something. Whether intentionally or not, he revealed that he knew Pia personally, enough for her to tell him something about me.

I need to know more. At least something worth bartering my life for. There has to be something from me he truly wants, something worth tolerating me. I doubt it's sex. So what?

He thinks I know of an Inglecias file my father kept, but I suspect that's only part of it.

Confronting him directly has been the only way I've made any headway with him. With one last look at the dress Ines selected for me, I inspect the closet, keeping that time frame at the back of my mind. *Ten minutes.* I can almost hear a clock ticking down, but when I reach for the nearest dress, I realize that the sound isn't entirely in my imagination.

I'm still wearing his watch on my wrist.

With it as my guide, I try to decide which outfit would best impress someone like him. *No.* That's the wrong way of looking at it. A better question is—what would best provoke him? Which of these would best rattle a man like Domino Valenciaga?

Someone who swears I disgust him, but has no problem utilizing my body to his own ends…

With time to spare, my gaze lands on the only dress to fit the bill. I snatch it and head for the bathroom. I dress as quickly as my aching limbs allow, and I barely manage to rinse out my mouth and run a damp rag over my skin before I head for the dining room.

It's overcast, and the lack of sunlight robs the house of its warmth. It's a cold, gray landscape now, with the wind lashing at the windows. Each one is closed today, and the doorway to the terrace is sealed by a set of white lattice doors.

Domino sits bathed in the near darkness of the dining room at the head chair. White curtains shroud the windows and the sight of the storm brewing beyond the trees.

"I see you're well rested," he says as I approach. "So am I—"
He sits up straighter, taking in my appearance with a swiping glance. I can practically smell his annoyance, heightening the strange spicy nature of his scent.

He doesn't call attention to my ensemble out loud, however.

"Sit," he demands, palming the table.

I do, inching toward the chair nearest to him. As I lower myself onto it, I know full well he's eyeing my clothing again, seething.

But it's a fragile victory.

This dress is the definition of dichotomy. Revealing and conservative at the same time. With a high, collared neckline and long, loose sleeves, it's damn near matronly compared to my usual outfits. Even Papa didn't specify such modesty with the style of clothing he picked for me.

But despite its form, the material of this dress is reminiscent of tissue paper. Thin enough to see through, catching glimpses of everything from the curls between my legs, to the darker colored flesh around my nipples.

As well as the scabbed, bloodied patches of skin.

I know the sight of it all bothers him. I chose well.

Sighing, he claps, summoning a single server who sets a platter of food in the center of the table. Much like yesterday, it contains an array of fruit and bite-sized pieces of bread and cheese.

Which isn't fair. I'm used to being plied with extravagant meals from my parents' dining table on plates so large it's child's play to make it look like I've eaten while resisting a single bite.

He changes the battlefield, picking food items that put the control in his hands. I can't fake my way out of it, and…

I'm so damn hungry it physically hurts. Gritting my teeth can't distract from it, and I realize that it's harder to resist him if the benefits aren't the same. He won't ignore my denial much longer, and for the first time I'm wary of just how long he'll let me deny him.

Another server appears with a bottle of blood-colored wine and two glasses.

Once we're alone, Domino gestures to the spread. "Eat. Though, since you're dressed as a nun, perhaps you aim to lead us in a prayer first? By all means. I assume you've been praying for bravery, because you've certainly become so brazen overnight. Attacking me. Crawling into my bed. And now you shamelessly brandish that which you've stolen from me—" he nods to my wrist and the watch I'm still wearing.

I swallow hard, knowing that my next words alone will convey the most impact. I can't threaten him, or ignore this slight, either. I have to provoke him.

"Since you plan on selling me, I didn't want you to be tempted any further," I say. Then I remember something I overheard. He'd been on the phone, I think?

I've let you keep your toy…

"I wouldn't want to cause another delay," I add, my throat so dry I swear I can feel it turn to dust and wither beneath the glare he shoots my way.

"Be careful before you get your wish," he warns. "Do you really think you're so sly that I don't see right through you?"

I shake my head. "I don't want you to see me at all."

It's a lie, of course. After five years of invisibility, I finally have his attention—and it's more addicting than I would have ever thought. The worst kind of drug, with a wider range of highs and lows than anything I've taken before.

To be fair, I've only experienced the lows—his anger, his rage, his loathing.

"You never told me what you wanted earlier," he says, his tone suddenly passive. He sits back in his chair while grabbing the wine bottle and an empty glass. Slowly, he nearly fills the entire goblet. Then he takes a sip.

"What I wanted?" I croak. His grin warns that I've stepped right into his trap.

"For being such a good girl and taking my cock like that."

I cringe, my face heating. With little effort, he's reset our dynamic, reinforcing that he's the only one with any real leverage to be had.

"They're going to love that, where you're going."

"Where, exactly?" I risk asking. A name floats through my thoughts, too faint to grab. Something about a tiger…

"A place where girls like you enter and never come out again."

It's the first time he's explicitly alluded to what being "sold" really means in the grand scheme, for me anyway—death. I should be terrified by the prospect. But I'm not. There are so many worse things than dying—all of which I might endure at this place, wherever it is. The unknown is more alarming than anything else. A pathetic thought gnaws away at my resolve. I want to go home.

"How far away is it?" I ask, resigned.

He takes another measured sip. "Far."

"When am I leaving?"

"You should have some wine." His deeper inflection warns that it wasn't a friendly request. He snatches the empty glass and fills it himself, placing it before me. "I think you'll find it's your favorite vintage."

I shiver at the bold claim, alarmed that he might be right. The bottle's label is deliberately turned, so I can't see it. Warily, I grab the glass, inhaling the liquid within. It doesn't smell poisoned. I take the smallest sip and wince.

He's right.

"A damn fine year. You have your father's taste to thank for that."

"You know me so well?"

His brows knit together, conveying suspicion. "There is a difference in knowing someone, and that someone being simplistic enough to understand, Ada-Maria."

The insult strikes true. He thinks I'm shallow enough to require the minimal effort to outsmart. Why not prove him right by responding with the most predictable answer.

"I know you," I say.

He laughs. "I'm sure you *think* you do." He takes another sip and washes it down with a grape fished from the platter. "Eat. Or not. I think I'll enjoy shoving the feeding tube down your throat when you're conscious."

I smother a gasp at the admission. "*You* did it?"

"You sound so surprised." He smirks, setting his wine aside. "And I thought you knew me so well."

"Were you medically trained?" I ask, taking a stab in the dark. "Or was that one of the torture skills you learned while working for my father?"

"No." His mouth falls into a rigid, hard line. "You could say I learned it indirectly as a result of the actions of Don Roy, though."

"Why do you still call him that?"

"Don?" He chuckles softly to himself, shaking his head. "I didn't realize you were never in on the joke."

"Enlighten me then," I dare him.

"It was a moniker his enemies cooked up to strengthen the rumors they spread about him working closely with the cartels. Mostly true rumors, mind you. Don is the title bestowed upon mob leaders, and your father proudly took up that name in a mocking salute to dispel the bad press and prove that he had nothing to hide. Perhaps I call him that out of respect."

"Why work so long for someone you hated? You lived with us. Ate with us. My mother gave you cufflinks for Christmas and invited you to sit at our bench during mass. My father trusted you."

"Trust means nothing to a man like Don Roy," Domino counters. "It's as fickle as currency. Mine was always too steep a price for a bastard like him to afford."

"So from the start, you were working against him," I deduce.

"And again, Ada-Maria, you prove that you are not as dumb as you look."

"No," I argue. "I'm far, far more stupid. I actually thought you were someone of integrity. The one man I could admire in a world of cutthroats and scoundrels. Thank you for proving to me that all men are the same—worthless bastards."

He should smirk, but that frown doesn't budge. "You didn't admire your father? Say it isn't so. You certainly had me fooled."

I look away. The wine glass is in my hand again, and I slosh some onto my dress in my haste to take a sip. A pull. Greedily, I drain the glass in one go.

"Careful," Domino spits. "You know that's no Kool-Aid you're drinking."

He sounds damn near disapproving. Still, as I set my empty glass down, I'm hungrily eyeing the bottle, wondering if I have the gall to pour more myself.

Get a grip, Ada! I shake my head, inhaling deeply. What did he say? A quip about my father.

"Maybe you don't know *me* so well after all," I counter. Too late do I realize from his fearsome grin that I've given him exactly what he wants—an opening to attack.

"Maybe I don't," he admits, appraising me with another searching glance. He lingers over my throat. Glancing down, I spot the scarlet stain there, gluing the fabric to my skin. "Those marks on your back. Were those from your father?"

I flinch and look away, biting my lip. *Shit!* I can't let him unnerve me like this. Belatedly, I get ahold of my senses enough to toss back, "I think they're from *you*."

"No. Before that. Don't play coy. Do you need a reminder?" I hear the quiet commotion as he stands. His presence disrupts the entire atmosphere of the room. Freed from his weight, the chair squeals in relief. The shadows stretching across the floor grow longer, with his bulk choking out what little light remains. When he comes up behind me, my entire body tenses—a reaction he is well aware of as he slides his hands around my shoulders, finding the button at the top of my collar.

"Let's refresh your memory, and mine. Get up."

He doesn't give me the chance to refuse or comply. He grips the dress' thin material and tugs until I have no choice but to stagger to my feet. Slowly, he undoes the next button. The next. The next…

I eye the wall as he exposes my breasts to the empty room. If a thousand men were here watching, I doubt I'd feel any more demeaned. They would lust after my body, at least, and be disgusted by my wounds.

He craves both. His low hum of appreciation sets my skin on fire with a crippling mixture of shame and…excitement? It's close to how he sounded on the verge of release, but this time he's merely peeling my dress down my arms, exposing my raw, ripped back.

He leaves the fabric hanging loosely from my hips and grips my shoulders, urging me down until I'm bending at the waist with my front pressed against the table's surface.

"I can tell the difference between old scars and new," he breathes out, ghosting his hand down my sides, grazing the bones of my ribcage as he goes. "These are very old. A few years at least."

Ten, to be exact. Newer ones were easier to have removed, but those were too deep. Too stubborn.

"These were made with more than just plain leather…" He runs the width of his thumb across my lower back as if reading the trauma simply by feel. "Metal tails. Or a spur."

"You sound impressed," I rasp, hating the quiver in my voice. I'm gazing up at the bottle of wine just beyond my reach, desperate for a sip.

"These weren't done to punish you," he continues as if I never spoke. "This was cruel. Harsh. If I were to whip you this way now, I could kill you."

He doesn't sound alarmed by that. My breathing feathers, and I squeeze my eyes shut, trying to ignore why my pulse quickens at that, my inner thighs shaking, my sore throat dampening…

"This hurt you," Domino surmises, withdrawing his touch, leaving me shivering in the aftermath. "Though I think you enjoy pain."

I bite my lip harder, remembering the way he whipped me. I didn't enjoy that.

"The right kind of pain," he corrects as if reading my mind. "Tell me who hurt you and why."

We both know the answer to at least one of those questions. But I forget my plan for manipulation in favor of giving in to the angry impulse to deny him.

"I will never tell you. Ever."

He growls. Or maybe that low series of notes was meant to resemble a laugh? His teeth are bared in a snarl fearsome enough to provide evidence for both theories.

Moving from my position, he grabs his half-empty wine glass and refills it. To my shock, he tops up mine as well.

"I'm sure we could come to an arrangement. I can think of several ways to coax an answer out of you." The malice in his voice sends ripples of alarm down my spine. "Oh, but what was that I promised?—" He inclines his glass toward me and sips from the rim. "To treat you sweetly, like a goddamn princess."

He slams his glass down, splashing liquid over his fingers and the table. The vivid splotches glimmer in the dim lighting, reminiscent of blood.

"I am to coddle you," he adds as a slow smile plays on his mouth. "So, what will it be? A bath by candlelight? A massage? Having me hand-feed you grapes as you lounge in bed?"

His guttural tone takes each suggestion and twists it to imply something nefarious. He'll hurt me, hurt me, or hurt me.

"I want you to give me answers," I suggest. "Why take me? Why now? What do you want? What do you think my father did to Pia? How do you know her—"

"I have a better suggestion."

He's behind me in a heartbeat, palming my lower back with both hands, grinding his touch into the marks beneath.

White-hot pain shoots through me. For a second, I see stars. Then blackness. It feels like ages before the world returns in full focus, though it must be mere seconds. He's still speaking. "I could fuck you senseless right here and now. You seem to respond well to that."

Panic grips me. I can't lose what little leverage I already have. So, I blurt, "A b-bath."

He stills, his breathing heavy. "Good choice. Ines," he calls, raising his voice. "Ada-Maria would like a candlelit bath. Run one in the jacuzzi. Bring out the rose petals. We'll make it fit for a queen."

He's mocking me again, and I suspect it's more than my impertinent questions that has him aggravated so. Something that's gnawing away at him, lurking behind those dark eyes. So he lashes out.

My only method to catch him off guard has been to play along. And make him break his own mold he's put me in.

"I...I want music," I say, a random request that gets his attention. He looks at me again, an eyebrow raised skeptically.

"Music it is," he says to my shock. "What kind?"

"I..."

"My choice, then," he declares, latching onto my hesitation. "Anything else?"

Yes, my instinct tells me. I need to keep him focused on me, anticipating my next action.

"Yes. I want wine. And…"

"And sweets, let's not forget the refreshments," he says, taking a step toward me to press his palm against my cheek. "I'll need you well rested and well fed for what I have planned for you. Despite what you may believe, cum is not fitting sustenance in the long-term, Ada."

Bastard. My cheeks flush with blood, but I hold his stare and nod.

"And… I w-want—"

"Such a greedy girl." He coaxes my chin higher, exposing my sore throat. Flashing dangerously, his eyes rake over the swollen flesh, and I realize my mistake—I've provoked him too much. "You want a more suitable item of clothing to wear," he adds softly. "Something more fitting than this matronly garb, *si*?"

I swallow hard and remain silent, having learned my lesson.

"Excellent," he murmurs. "Then what are we waiting for?"

CHAPTER SEVENTEEN

His room contains its own private balcony, through a door I missed on my earlier visits. Open to the night air, it's a wide space, shrouded by more trees and hedges—as well as an extension of the roof that protects us from the light rain beginning to fall.

Built into a raised platform near the balcony is a bubbling jacuzzi, arranged to his chilling specifications.

Rose petals coat the stone patio, tinging the air with the sickly-sweet scent. Soft music plays from unseen speakers, the tune light, featuring a male singer crooning in Spanish. Steam emanates from the bathwater, and along the rim, someone laid out a black, crushed velvet blanket strewn with red cushions. Placed in the center is a golden tray sporting various sweets, from cakes, to cookies, and pieces of chocolate.

It's terrifying how he can arrange something like this at a moment's notice. It shows the level of resources he has at his disposal. But how?

"So much fresh fruit," I say thickly. "But you said we're miles from any city."

Or any supermarket capable of supplying the amount he's paraded before me. I doubt he sends Ines on regular supply runs, either.

He's behind me, his breath hot on my neck. I rebuttoned my dress for the trip here, but he's already reaching around me to undo them, one by one.

"The estate is self-sustaining," he replies. "Most of the fruit and vegetables are grown here. The rest has been stocked well in advance, so if you're planning on seducing some charming delivery man into whisking you to safety, I would think again."

I smother my disappointment beneath a sigh. He already has me partially naked, tugging the dress down my hips.

"It's my turn to ask the questions." He palms my waist, guiding me forward. Only belatedly does he seem to remember my bandages. He fingers one along my forearm then withdraws his hand.

The second I hear the telltale hiss of leather on metal, I stiffen, already aware of what he's doing without having to look. I didn't even realize that he had his knife, dangling from that battered sheath affixed to his belt loop. He presses the flat side of the blade to my skin in a shockingly cool caress. Slowly, he guides it down, catching the edge of a section of bandages. It easily slices apart, falling away.

"You have such delicate skin," he remarks, cutting through a strip of bandages along my thigh next. "I have to take special care with you. I wouldn't want you to boil alive in the bath."

He keeps going, clearing the next wrapping around my left elbow before crouching down to clear away the ones on my feet.

The wounds beneath glisten, a pale pink. None of them are deeper than a few layers of skin, most resembling blisters formed after a bad sunburn.

"Don't worry," Domino says, rising to his feet. He smooths my hair down my shoulders, tucking a stray lock behind my ear. "I've taken precautions with the water's quality to ensure you won't risk an infection. I would never take the chance of you dying such an easy death, Ada."

A breath sticks inside my chest. It's several tries before I can suck in enough air.

"Is that why you went after me?"

I can almost hear the muscles in his jaw straining as he frowns. He doesn't like that insinuation. Roughly, he snatches my wrist, wrenching me around to face him. One of his fingers grazes my skin, settling against my throat.

"I went after you, because I own you."

He's lying. I can hear the subtle growl edging those words. Irritation.

"You don't, do you?" I rasp, recalling a name Ines said. The speaker on the telephone. "J-Jaguar? Does he own me?"

His eyes flash, and I have my answer. It's horrifying, proving that all along, his taunts have been true. He sold me. Maybe, deep down, a part of me refused to believe it. For five years, this man pretended to be willing to lay down his life to guard my father and me. Was it all truly a lie?

I don't want to think anymore. I don't want to fight or resist him. I'm too tired. I just want to sink inside myself and sleep. Burrow beneath the blankets in that white room and endure the remaining hours I have left.

"I've decided that a week and some change is not nearly enough to divulge from you all that I want, Ada-Maria," Domino warns.

The pure malice in his tone snaps me from my self-pity. I'm on edge again, painfully aware of his darker intentions. If I needed a reminder, he trails his hands down my back, carelessly running over the healing wounds.

"I want you to keep that in mind, no matter what you perceive to be happening at any given time. On your father's behalf, you owe me far more than could ever be paid in a lifetime, even with money. You owe me blood, Ada. I aim to take every last drop from you, in whichever way I choose."

The sheer weight of the promise in his voice is dizzying. He means every word—no matter how badly they contradict everything else he's stated up until now.

"How?" I demand. "You've already sold me. I'm not yours anymore… Not that I ever was."

He chuckles, urging me forward with a surprisingly gentle nudge.

"Your bath water is getting cold."

He makes me climb in by myself as he watches.

The water is hot, though nowhere near the searing heat he taunted me with last time. Still, I suck in a breath, hissing in agony as the water contacts the open sores on my feet and legs. I go rigid, anticipating the pain to last.

But it's brief, perhaps due to the gently swirling jets and whatever he must have added to the water. It smells faint but crisp like flowers. Soon, my torso is nearly submerged, leaving just my shoulders and up exposed.

I wait for Domino to squeeze into what little space remains. To my shock, he stretches out on the black blanket, picking at some of the items on the platter.

He's stripped his pants, wearing only a pair of black boxers, but his loose-fitting white shirt remains firmly in place, the top two buttons undone.

"You don't ever show your chest," I point out warily. Looking back, I realize that I can't name a single time I ever saw him in less than a buttoned shirt or the occasional wife beater. Could he have gruesome scars he's trying to hide? I doubt modesty is the reason.

Raising a grape to his lips, he takes a bite. "I would be more concerned with preserving your own beautiful skin than worrying about mine."

Point taken. I'm more than willing to stare down at the churning water or beyond the balcony than watch him. We're high up despite the house seemingly being all one level. This section of the property dips into a startlingly steep hill that puts into question any possibility of sneaking back here and trying to climb down.

Not that I would have to go to such lengths to escape, anyway. I've already walked out of the front door twice. Beyond this strange, lush realm is only desert.

The amount of water needed to sustain the gardens, let alone a supposed farm, must be astronomical.

"Were you able to buy this place with whatever you made by selling me?" I ask, daring to look at him again.

"I've always had my own means," he says. "Long before I toiled away for your father, doing his dirty work for scraps."

I say nothing, thinking back to the first day he arrived at the guesthouse. His truck had been a decade old, his clothing worn, all able to fit in a single suitcase. I remember being in awe of him for that, such a modest man from a humble background. I thought that made him different from my father, who prized his expensive possessions and expansive estate.

How wrong I was, especially if Domino owned this estate that entire time. It's larger than my father's, just in sheer size alone.

"Perhaps that explains your newfound obsession with my cock," he adds, fingering another lock of my hair. "You realized that I'm not some poor bastard living off your father's teat."

I cringe from his touch. "I always wanted you. Before," I clarify. "I didn't care that you had nothing."

And I didn't. Money to me was always an obscure concept, anyway. My father had it—not me.

"And now?" Domino asks. He sounds curious as to the answer, but I take my time devising one. How best to provoke him?

"I wanted to know if you were worth obsessing over for five years."

He scoffs. "And?"

I look down at the water, weighing my answer. Insulting him is the most obvious retort, but it's too easy—and exactly what he's expecting, I think. So I tell the truth instead.

"You aren't who I thought you were." And that saddens me deeply. I'm used to being disappointed in people, but Domino was admittedly my benchmark for so long…

It's a little like going to heaven and learning that Jesus snorts cocaine and has a gambling addiction, no different from the rest of us. Not that I ever thought Domino Valenciaga was quite on that level. But in a world of men populated by my father, he might as well have been.

"And who did you think I was?"

I shy from the real answer, but it isn't like I have anything left to lose. Meeting his gaze, I decide that this perhaps is the best way to keep provoking him. With the past.

"Someone I could love," I say. It sounds so juvenile out loud, though maybe it should. I'm utilizing Pia's logic and the future she always saw for me. Someone desired. Obsessed over. A woman who could dare to find true love.

"And what did I do to garner such an esteemed view in the eyes of Ada-Maria Pavalos?" His tone is disapproving. Skeptical. He doesn't believe me.

I sink deeper beneath the churning water until it sloshes at my chin. What did Domino do then that stuck out to me so? I ignore the man he is now, seeing past the cruel hard gaze for the vulnerable warmth I used to swear lurked beneath.

"You dragged me from the road in the middle of the night and never told my father. He would have beaten me senseless for that. Not because he cared, but because I might have been seen by someone else, and how would that look? He would have given you a handsome raise, I bet. Or you could have extorted what you wanted from me. I would have done anything to keep you quiet. And you knew that,"

I add before he tries to play dumb. "You knew him better than anyone. Don't pretend like you didn't."

"And if I did, I'd know that he wouldn't want to be bothered with tales of his drunk, coke-addicted daughter taking a nap on the freeway—"

"Don't minimize it!" I'm shouting, my throat on fire. When I look at him, he has the gall to appear shocked by the outburst. "You could have left me there if you really didn't give a damn."

"No." He leans forward, bracing his elbow on the edge of the jacuzzi to prop his chin on his hand. "That is where you are wrong, Ada. I see it now. You never understood your true worth, did you? How could I leave Roy Pavalos' daughter, drugged out of her mind, unaccompanied in the middle of the road? Any number of enemies would have taken you for their own."

Just like he has.

Anger plays on my common sense, making me think of the pettiest way to provoke him. He thinks he owns me, does he?

"Whenever I get to my *real* owner, I'll make him an offer— he can do whatever he wants to me. Just so long as he leaves me in the middle of the highway after—"

"Now it's my turn to warn you not to minimize." Domino snatches my chin, tilting it for his inspection. "You think this is a game? You have no idea what one of those men is capable of. Trust me, Ada-Maria. After one night, your entire time here will look like a trip to the spa."

I don't flinch. "You act as though this is new to me, Domino. But it's not. Cruel men and senseless brutality? You are just one in a long line of them. Trust me, I'm looking forward to this new place. I'll pray for a man who won't hit me on the face and feel I've won the lottery—"

Water splashes as he lunges into the tub, still wearing boxers and his shirt. Drenched, the fabric molds to his muscle-like armor as he yanks me to my feet.

"You want to know the kind of men you'll meet there? Men who will chop you into pieces—I'm talking literally, Ada. As they fuck you, knives stabbed right into your skin. They'll sic ten of them on you at once and gladly feed the pieces to the animals they keep there in cages, right next to the women. Still, sound preferable to me?"

I blink, startled by the tears that slip down my cheeks. The worst part is that I know he isn't lying. He's done this to me. He's condemned me to that fate.

And for what?

Growling with rage, he digs his nails into my jawline. "You didn't answer my question—"

"Yes! Yes, I'd prefer anyone to you! Because I hate you. I do. And even being eaten alive, I'll at least be comforted by the fact that I'll never have to see your face again."

Hearing that bothers him. I can see the rage boiling beneath his skin until he can't contain it. He shoves me back so fiercely I wind up sitting on the rim of the tub, bracing myself with both hands. As a result, I cannot defend myself as he advances, boldly nudging himself between my legs.

"You sneer down your nose at me, Ada, but I know who you are. A nasty, backstabbing little trollop-whore."

That word choice…

My eyes widen, my shock apparent. Only one person I knew ever spoke like that.

"P-Pia—"

"She told me all about you," Domino says coldly. He encircles both of his hands around my throat, forming a makeshift collar. "How sneaky you are. How untrustworthy. That you fed her to the wolves and made her life hell." He tightens his grip, pressing against my windpipe. "She told me everything I need to know about you, Ada-Maria Pavalos—that beneath that beautiful exterior, that haughty pout, and those limpid fucking eyes, you are a cunt, far more evil than even your father. Roy did what he did to protect his money. But you? You were a conniving bitch merely out of jealousy."

"Pia told you that?" I can barely get the words out.

He nods, stroking the falling tears from my cheeks. "Yes. She told me—"

"And did she tell you *why* I hated her?" I'm whispering. It's as if my own body is doing everything it can to resist unearthing these memories. I've spent so long ignoring them, smothering them, hating myself.

And yet Pia, wherever she is, has been laughing over it all, toying with the truth, turning men I barely know against me.

"Pia was a whore."

He moves to slap me, as if the impulse to protect even her name is that damn strong. But I don't cringe. I wait for the impact, so hard I see stars.

I cough, tasting blood as I stagger, forced to grip the bench hidden beneath the water just to keep my head above it. Meeting his gaze, I spit.

"She was… Pia was fucking my father. Did she tell you that? She was never my friend. I… I was only a tool to her. She used me. Just like everyone else did."

CHAPTER EIGHTEEN

He blinks, his hand still raised as if he intends to strike me again. I recoil this time, holding my hands before my face in a pathetic attempt to protect it.

"You're lying."

It's my turn to laugh, frothing at the mouth as I do. He hit me hard enough to split my lip, and the blood drips freely. "How do you think she got access to steal from us in the first place? My bedroom wasn't where my father kept his accounts; it was in his office."

The same office where I would catch her scent on the days she told me she was too busy to hang out after school. The same office where my father would work late. I wasn't sure until she wore a ring she said her secret boyfriend had given her.

It was my mother's. I didn't realize that until later, of course, after things with Pia had already reached a boiling point.

"She was fucking him," I add tonelessly, "and she tried blackmailing my family when he grew bored of her. She was never my friend. She never loved me. It was always him."

For everyone, it's always *him*. Don Roy. Roy Pavalos. Until the day someone did something as simple as dragging me from a highway in the middle of the night without asking for a damn thing in return.

"You were the only person who didn't treat me like a way to get to him! I thought you were…"

And it guts me to realize how stupid a hope that was. How childish.

"All along, you were just like them. Like Pia. Like everyone!"

I shove him away and climb from the tub, tripping over my own feet. My eyes are on the balcony, and I lunge for it, leaning over the railing. I eye the darkened landscape below. I'm not afraid. I don't feel anything, and in this moment…

I know for sure I could jump.

Fall.

"Are you fucking crazy?" A masculine arm comes around my waist, wrenching me back.

"No!" Blindly, I lash out, striking whatever part of him I can reach. None of my blows do a damn thing. He's immovable. As impenetrable as a brick wall. "Let me go!"

He doesn't, gripping my entire body within a bear hug so that I can't fight. All I can do is scream, no matter how painful it is, until my voice breaks and I can't even make a sound.

But as I fall silent, I realize that he's still speaking to me. He always has been.

"…you walk around with your nose in the fucking air. How could I think you were any different?" The words are meant more for him than me, I realize. With my face pressed against his chest, I can hear how fiercely his heart is raging. A near-constant boom that rattles his ribcage.

"The dumb whore with a heart of gold—no one fits that fucking cliché. No one…"

He's trying to justify it, I think. Why it was so easy for him to believe Pia about someone he hadn't even met. All along, he's thought the worst of me, lies planted by my old best friend.

"How could I ever think any bastard who would work for my father could be any different?" My voice is so hoarse I'm sure he doesn't hear that.

Regardless, he looks down, his eyes sharp and mistrusting. He adjusts his grip, loosening his bear hug to grip me by both forearms, holding me captive inches from his chest. When he lunges, I go still, expecting another slap.

Not the feel of his mouth over mine.

He's brutal, gnashing with his teeth until I part my aching lips and let him in. He grunts, gripping me tighter, pressing me against the planes of his chest. Using his weight as a battering ram, he jolts me back, forcing me to step down into the tub.

I can see the intention written across his face as he pulls back, tugging at the front of his boxers.

I don't resist, letting him spin me around and manipulate my body until I'm standing in the tub, leaning over the edge with my hands braced before me.

One thrust, and he's deep, sending the water sloshing between us. I close my eyes, surrendering to each thrust. It's a brutal rhythm that's somehow gentler than the roughness of the other night.

His hand cinches my hair, his mouth against my ear. "For so fucking long, I've wanted you," he growls. "Always you…"

He's lying, I know he is. But that knowledge doesn't dull the effect those grated words have on my body. Nerves I didn't even know existed ignite and smolder. My breath quickens, my bones turning liquid beneath his touch.

He makes me chase after him, grinding against his hardness to salvage my own pleasure as he selfishly takes. Right when my breaths feather and eyelids flutter, his hand snakes down my front, dipping beneath the water, grinding against the sensitive flesh between my thighs.

He's ruthless, as if he studied how to touch me. Pleasure me.

Break me.

I never stood a damn chance.

WE WIND up on the blanket, the platter kicked aside, scattering the food all over the black material. He's on his back, his eyes on the overhang that shields this part of the terrace from a fresh bout of rain. I doubt it could protect us from lightning, but he doesn't seem worried.

I am.

Harsh, mindless sex I can stomach—not this. Whatever this is. Something more than physical, as foreign to me as it seems to be to him.

To break the silence, all I can think to say is, "Where is she?" Pia. He claimed she was dead, but obviously, she's not if she's able to feed him intel on me. Lies.

He tilts his head to shoot me a searching glance. Whatever he finds makes him frown and look away, turning his attention to the sky. "She's dead, Ada."

"Then how—"

"She never told me a damn thing herself."

So, he lied or made it up. It's cruel. But it doesn't match, unless he had another reason for hating me other than using a dead girl as his proxy.

"Your father killed her," he says tiredly. "I know he did."

"How?" I demand, slamming my hand against the stone tiles.

He stands, heading for the doorway. "I don't know how," he admits. "Or when. Or where…"

He enters the room but, just as I stand to follow, he reappears, holding a small object in his hands.

"But you are going to help me find the answers to those questions." He offers the object to me, and I sway.

It's a pink book, decorated in a multitude of stickers that were in fashion a decade ago. A name is written in a pink gel pen across a white label stuck to the front of it.

This diary belongs to: *Pia Alicia Inglecias*.

The last time I held this very book, I gave it to my father. "H-How?"

"That's not important. What matters is that Pia wrote about her 'favorite place' where she would hide her secrets. Where?"

I shrug. It's been so long, and Pia was known for her elusive word games. A favorite place could mean anything from the beach, to the ice cream parlor, to her favorite park bench.

"You know exactly what I'm talking about," Domino says, but it's not an accusation. He tosses the book onto the blanket before me. "You've read it, haven't you?"

How could I not? My father tasked me to steal it, but I needed to know why. And I needed to see exactly what my old friend thought of me.

And she hated me. I bored and annoyed her from the very start. I was an amusing pet to play with when she needed someone. The way she spoke about me...

It was vicious. Cruel. But still generally polite in Terra Rodea standards. After all these years, I think I should despise her. I still don't. She wasn't like me, and that was another layer of her appeal. She was poor, forced to navigate the world without a powerful last name.

But there was one person she did care about—enough to justify her stealing and backstabbing. Enough to justify her scheming ways.

Slowly, I look up to find Domino still watching me, his shirt even more out of place now that his bottom half is completely bare.

"Take it off," I rasp. "Take off your shirt."

His eyes narrow, and I expect him to refuse. Instead, he snatches the hem, balling it. By the time he drags the material over his head, I've already seen the glaring proof I needed to cement my suspicion.

"You're Navid." Pia's brother, stricken with a heart condition —only the harsh scar slicing in between his pecs reveals how he managed to circumvent that ailment. He must have had a transplant, years before he joined my father.

And so many things start to click.

Greed was never his motivation. Just revenge.

And that makes him far more dangerous.

"I imagined this," he says with a harsh scoff as he flicks his wadded shirt aside. "You, gaping up at me on your knees, whimpering my name like it's some fucking revelation."

My performance must not satisfy him. He climbs into the tub and sits, tilting his head back against the rim to watch me.

"You hated us all this time," I croak. "So what? By killing my parents and selling me, you get some sick, twisted enjoyment out of it?"

He raises an eyebrow. "This is about far more than a silly tit-for-tat, Ada-Maria," he says. "Far more than just revenge. You only factor in as a very small part. This was never about just *you*."

"How?" I demand, drawing my knees up to my chest, feeling the exposed wounds smart and sting. No matter the discomfort, it feels important to shroud myself from him. It doesn't matter that he's already experienced nearly every inch of my body.

He doesn't own me.

"I'll tell you—the price you'll fetch is more than enough to square away some old debts of mine. Nothing more, nothing less."

It's a gut punch. He says it so casually. So callously. That's all I ever was to him. A bargaining chip.

"Debts," I whisper. "To Jaguar?"

"I wouldn't go around parroting names and terms I didn't understand, were I you. In the real world, Ada, a name is a man's most important possession. He'll do anything to protect it, even kill."

"Which is why you spent five years living under a false identity, *Domino*," I point out.

"I am Domino Valenciaga. Any prior name I may have had is no longer relevant. Disrespect it, and I'll teach you firsthand how these disputes are settled by those without a rich father to hide behind."

"My father taught me that respect is earned," I counter.

He leans back as if relishing the feel of the jets. "You only say that because you think I won't lunge from this tub and wrap my hands around that pretty throat. Respect is a term beyond any Pavalos."

I flinch, stung. Again, I want nothing more than to flee. Run. Hide. Jump off the balcony and end my suffering now. I can't take another moment with him. I can't.

"Come." As if reading my mind, he beckons me with a dripping finger. "Join me."

It's both a dare and a test.

His eyes gleam mischievously as I comply, sinking onto the submerged bench across from him. Our legs intertwine, and I cringe at the sensation. He's both firm and unmoving, like living metal, his limbs serving as makeshift bars to this newer prison.

"Tell me something," he demands. "You keep pouting every time I voice my assessment of you. You are what you are, Ada. But let's hear from the little princess why she may have some depth."

He can be so unbearably mean. His words, at times, cut deeper than even the leather of his whip.

"I loved you because I thought you were someone of integrity. Not perfect—" I add before he can interject.

No, Domino was never perfect.

"But someone who could think for himself. Who supported my father for his own reasons—" And in a way, I was right all along. "But a man who could determine on his own what was right and wrong. Someone with enough honor to ignore his attraction to any woman who might interfere with his duties. I especially loved that."

I'm not ashamed to reminisce over this fictional Domino. In a sense, it's freeing. Let him hear all the lofty standards he never lived up to. Though, I figure, no man could.

"I thought you were loyal and brave. I thought you were fair. Fair enough to save my life and ask for nothing in return. You could have extorted me a million times over, if all you wanted was money."

"This is about more than money, Ada," he finally says after letting me speak.

I fling open my eyes, exasperated. "Then why sell me?"

"Blood debts require a more nuanced currency to satisfy," he says, once again resorting to word games. "Even the Bible provides its own rough description. An eye for an eye. A tooth for a tooth. A heart for a heart…"

And a woman for a girl.

This is about Pia—but on whose behalf does he seek to satisfy this invisible debt? His eyes are so emotionless, I can't tell.

"This is more than merely personal, either. Try as you might, you will never understand it. What a pity to shatter the lofty image you've built up for me."

He sounds mocking enough, his sly grin firmly fixed on his face.

But he's angry. I can see it in his glinting eyes and how stiffly he holds himself. I've struck a nerve. If only I knew which one.

"I'm used to being disappointed," I say softly. "Another reason you are just like my father—"

"I am nothing like him!" He's on me before I can react, his hand around my throat, forcing my back to arch as he leans over me. One of his hands feels out along the rim of the tub, returning with an item that he presses against my lips.

"Open."

His commanding tone is too fierce to resist.

I pry my lips apart, steeling my body for a horrific taste. Instead, a richness floods my tongue, conveying a flavor I haven't tasted in years. Chocolate. Insanely good dark chocolate with some kind of fruit filling to balance the salty bitterness.

"I prefer your mouth stuffed full," Domino warns, reaching for another sweet. Some kind of truffle that he dangles between two fingers. "I could keep you forever like this."

My ears pick up at the word choice. Is that his way of hinting that he won't sell me after all? A hateful mixture of hope and dread washes over me. As much as I try to tell myself that any fate is preferable to him, I know better…

I can't focus on the *what-ifs*. So, I just fixate on the potentials. If I could manipulate him into keeping me, what else could I make him do? It could be a slow, painful process, but one I think I could decipher if I tried hard enough. A somewhat known entity is far better than the unknown.

With my eyes on the chocolate, I choke down any hesitation and stick out my tongue, allowing him to place the morsel onto it. I chew slowly, hating the feeling of the chocolate and sugar disintegrating.

He watches, his curiosity piqued. He doesn't know what I'll do next, and there's power in those heavy few seconds before I finally lick my lips and say, "I could be yours alone. Why share me?"

Share. That word makes his nostrils flare, and I have my answer—he doesn't really want to. Not out of concern but greed. Jealousy. He's right. There's more to this than I'm aware of, and the thought terrifies the hell out of me.

It makes me reckless. Reckless enough to eye him through my lashes and soften my voice.

"I could be good to you."

"Little Ada," he taunts, bringing his thumb to my mouth next. He rams the pad of it between my lips, chuckling when I wince. "So good at the sexy mind games. No wonder your father sent you to assist with all his dirty work."

I let the barb pass unchallenged, keeping my focus on what matters.

"When is Jaguar coming for me, then?" I make my voice as weak and feeble as possible, even as I'm forced to speak around his probing thumb. "I could show him how good I can be with my mouth. Maybe he'll keep me—"

"He will *never* fucking touch you." Anger explodes from him, and I recoil. Seconds pass before I realize he just withdrew his hand. He never struck me. "Not if I have any say in that. I'll rip you to pieces if you even let him look at your body. Don't think I won't."

He's shaking, his hands in fists, eyes blazing. Slowly, he deflates. That display wasn't for my benefit. For once, I slipped beneath those barriers to the man beneath. Seething and jealous of this Jaguar and what he may or may not have.

Me.

I dull myself to the little voice at the back of my mind warning me not to and place my hand on his forearm, sensing the coiling, lethal muscle.

"If you don't want to sell me," I whisper, utilizing the same purr I'd employ to charm any other man in my orbit. "Keep me then."

And I can spend every waking moment afterward plotting my escape. Even if I have to drive that knife into his throat myself, I'll defeat him. I will.

He strokes my cheek and for a second, I think his guard is lowered enough for my ruse to work. "So eager to please. I like you better this way…" He leans forward, brushing his lips along my earlobe. "You think you have power. It's sexy."

I wince, concealing the act behind a smirk of my own. It feels hollow and lopsided, but I hold it for all I'm worth.

"I can have whatever you want me to," I parrot. "I can be whoever you want me to be. As long as you have me…"

His eyes flash at the subtle taunt.

He himself stated that fact won't be for long.

Unless, of course, he changes his mind.

Or rips me to pieces.

"You know what I want from you?" he asks in a tone that warns he'd very much like to enact the latter of my mental options. His finger flexes against my jawline as if best deciding where to start if he is planning on ripping me to pieces. Near my lip? My ear? Down along my throat? "I'll tell you one day. Preferably when you're less inclined to stab me with a hypodermic needle."

I grow cold at the reminder. Did he really plant that vial, knowing I'd take the risk to inject him with its contents? Looking at him, I can't tell and that unnerves me more than if he'd gloat over his plan outright.

"Why leave that stuff for me? Those pictures?" I demand.

He curls his fingers against my cheek, tilting it so that his mouth has better access to my ear. "To test you."

I feel my lips curl into a frown and I pull away from his touch. "And what's the verdict?" I ask nastily.

His laugh catches me by surprise, low and amused. Abruptly, he stands from the water and walks, dripping wet, into the bedroom.

I wait for my cue to follow, but it never comes. Apparently, though, our rare ceasefire is over. I don't know how I feel about that as I climb out of the water on my own and creep into the darkness of the room. I head for the hallway blindly—I'd rather leave naked than run the risk of him turning a request for a towel into another mind game.

With every step, my head is abuzz with too many questions to keep track of. His identity. Pia. My fate...

When I finally reach the door, I only hesitate at the thought of leaving the diary behind. In his hands, that tome from the past is a goldmine of information he can use against me.

"Did I say you could leave?" The gruff question comes from the direction of the bed. I didn't even realize Domino is already lying there, unabashedly naked over the neatly made sheets. Only the glow of the lights from the direction of the balcony gives him any definition against the shadows. "Come here."

I choke down a refusal and inch a step toward him, against my better judgment. One way to spin my obedience is that I can use this rare moment when he isn't coming at me with a whip or a collar to my advantage. Lure him into a false sense of security.

Though, as he snatches my wrist the second I'm within his reach, I realize that if anyone has let down their guard, it's me. I gasp as he drags me down until I'm practically on top of him. One of his hands claims my thigh and the heat basting my shoulder tells me that we're lying face to face, my breasts against his chest.

"I like you plotting and scheming," he murmurs in a tone that makes me shiver. "It bodes well for how you'll react when you see what it is a I really have in store for you."

A probing response is on my tongue, ready to be voiced. At the last second, I grit my teeth and remain silent.

He wants me angry and helpless—and I'll give him that and more.

Just on my own terms and on my timeline.

Even as I relax against him, I can tell he doesn't expect the way I sink into his touch, resting my head against his shoulder. The second he falls asleep, I'll sneak onto that balcony and grab the diary.

And I'll be the one capable of turning the tables then.

CHAPTER NINETEEN

I'm on top of him, though I don't remember making the decision to sleep here. On his bed. On his body. Naked.

It should feel far worse than it does, wrapped in a cocoon of a stormy, overcast morning and the semi-darkness of his bedroom.

Peace is a strange concept here. Maybe calm is a better word. The calm before the storm comes in the form of soft footsteps, and a gentle voice that pierces the quiet.

"Sir?"

"Goddamn." Domino hisses his irritation though he doesn't move. Because of me?

"Ines... What the hell? It's barely seven." He's taking pains with her that he doesn't usually, straining to keep his voice level, avoiding the use of any curse words. He respects her.

"I am sorry, sir. But Mr. Jaguar—"

"Tell him I'll call him later," Domino snaps.

Ines sighs. "I am sorry, sir. But Mr. Jaguar is *here*."

A WORD FROM THE AUTHOR

Hey there!

Thank you so much for reading! If you enjoyed the story, please leave a review and recommend the book to any friend you think would love this twisted world. You'd have my eternal gratitude. Even a short sentence goes a long way!

Then, come join the rest of us dark romance lovers in my Facebook Group where you can get snippets, sneak peeks of upcoming books and even help vote on aspects of future novels.

Come to the dark side:

https://www.facebook.com/groups/lanasbeautifulmonsters/

WANT MORE STUFF TO READ?
Join my newsletter and get a **free book**! Plus, you get to stay updated with any new releases, random giveaways and exclusive sneak peeks!
https://www.lanaskybooks.com/newsletter

Other Novels: https://lanaskybooks.com/

Lana Sky is a reclusive writer in the United States who spends most of her time daydreaming about complex male characters and parenting her Cockapoo Joey. She writes dark, twisted romance across several genres. Her titles include everything from mafia romance to vampires.

facebook.com/AuthorLanaSky

twitter.com/lanasky101

amazon.com/author/lanasky

pinterest.com/lanasky101

goodreads.com/lanasky

instagram.com/lanasky101

bookbub.com/authors/lana-sky

For more titles by Lana Sky, please visit:
https://www.lanaskybooks.com